Other Books by Dawn Greenfield Ireland

Nonfiction

The Puppy Baby Book

Writers Preparation
Handbook

Mastering Your Money

What's Breaking
Your Budget

Fiction

The Alcott Family Adventures

Hot Chocolate

Bitter Chocolate

Spicy Chocolate

Prophecy of Thol

The Last Dog

Coming soon:

Bonded

Gifts From Thol

Forced Dreams

Dawn Greenfield Ireland

An Artistic Origins Publication

Forced Dreams by Dawn Greenfield Ireland
Published by Artistic Origins Inc.

Copyright © 2018 Dawn Greenfield Ireland
All rights reserved.

Cover design by Marcha Fox / kallioperisingpress.com

Interior layout by Darwin Lopena / www.DarwinLopena.com

Planets by Fazila Rahat (faxila) Fiverr.com

ISBN 978-1-940385-14-3 (eBook)
ISBN 978-1-940385-15-0 (paperback)

Dawn Greenfield Ireland
www.dawngreenfieldireland.com

Please visit my website:
http://dawngreenfieldireland.com/

Sign up for my newsletter and get the latest news before the public.

The Planets

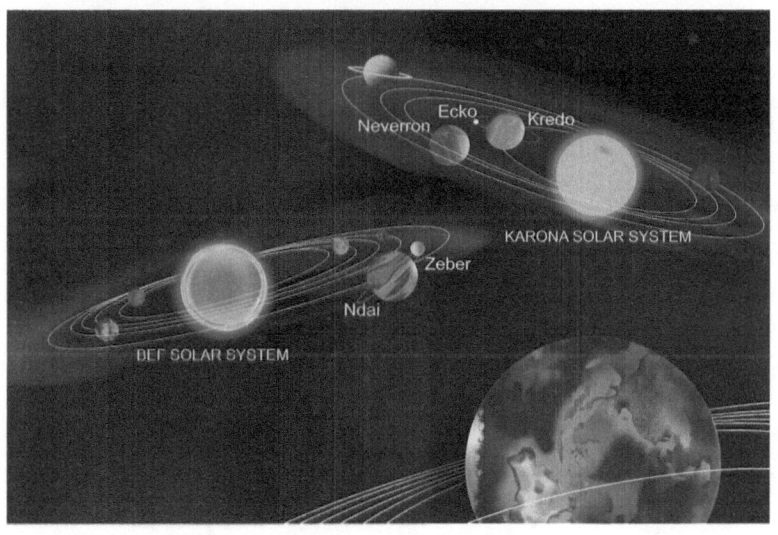

Table of Contents

Acknowledgements

Many thanks to Cicely Wynne, Anna Marie Fluche and Peggy Stautberg, my editors who carry big sticks. I get whacked so often people might suspect someone's abusing me.

I am grateful for my critique group for reading my pages and asking tough questions.

To all the people who follow me on Facebook, Twitter, LinkedIn and Instagram – my electronic friends and family who cheer me on through book after book, project after project – I couldn't do it without you.

Thanks to Marcha Fox for the fabulous front and back covers! She read the book and created the covers.

And a big cheer to my beta readers: Jake, Jeff, Linda, Dave, Laura, Sandy, Trudy and Joe. Your eyes took a beating. Thanks for making this book even stronger!

Thanks to Fazila Rahat (faxila) on Fiverr.com for the fabulous solar system drawing in the front of the book.

I would be in a world of hurt without Darwin Lopena, my secret weapon who formats all my eBooks and paperbacks. He's rescued my projects so many times I've lost track.

In Memory Of

Robert Williams and Will Schoggins

You left way too soon.

Chapter 1

Alma moaned from the sheer physical desire for him. His lips, mouth and hands sensually attacked her, sending spasms of pleasure throughout every part of her body, mind, and soul. The intense sensation devoured her mind, holding her in bondage.

Long auburn hair fanned out on the cool white sheets making a captivating picture on the huge antique oak spindle bed. The luxurious bedroom, decorated in peach and green, faded as passion burned through her.

Alma traced frantic patterns along his tanned, muscular arms and across his strong back as the onslaught of her senses continued. It was all she could manage—her mind was practically gone. Her fingers ran through his thick, blond hair down the sides of his neck to his powerful shoulders as he made love to her.

Her head rolled from side to side as his body moved along hers, allowing his lips and hands access to more delights. She couldn't stop herself from gasping, moaning.

"Mark." She woke with the name dangling on her lips, his features etched on her brain as an invaluable keepsake. She was soaking wet from the dream tryst, but her mouth was as dry as the desert. Her body tingled, alive with sensations from a night spent in his arms—or so it seemed.

The dream had been so real.

Was it a dream?

She questioned the validity of her doubt, no longer sure about anything. Reaching out, she touched the light blue sheets on her bed.

Only a dream; no luxury white sheets here, no antique bed.

She stared at the ceiling as she thought about the dream. Alma didn't know who he was, but she would recognize him in a crowd or on a busy street. He was tall and blond.

At first, she had assumed it was her late husband, Jeff. But those eyes weren't Jeff's—his had been soft and gentle, amber as tigers' eye. And, she admitted, Jeff's lovemaking was no comparison, except for the two times she conceived.

Mark's eyes were as blue as a summer sky, and she had never seen eyes that shade of blue before. They were startling, unsettling. When he looked at her with those eyes he gazed into her, saw everything—all her secrets.

Both men were built similarly, except Mark was chiseled with defined muscles, and his six-pack abs that Alma ran her hands over in the dream.

Jeff was much softer. How ghoulish to compare this man to her dead husband, but the similarity was uncanny.

This was the second week of the recurring dream. It hadn't started like this but had progressed to this stage through courtship and ritual. At first, he just appeared one night in a mixed-up dream where she was searching for an insignificant object. She couldn't even remember what it had been, but he found it and held it out to her. When their fingers touched, sparks flew, setting the embers blazing.

After that appearance he was around all the time. His seductions began with a look, sometimes a phrase, then a touch.

The turning point was his kiss—it had been the most erotic kiss she had ever experienced. Mark filled her with an erupting passion that threatened to burst her veins. She couldn't escape him, didn't want to escape him.

Oh, that feeling of being alive with sensations of uncontrollable passion!

There had never been anything so pleasurable or exciting in her entire life as the experiences in the dream.

Alma knew his voice, his hands, and his lips by heart. She knew his thoughts as he knew hers. They were the most intimate of lovers, going beyond physical love, merging their bodies and souls.

She wasn't sure how a dream could weave your mind inside out, but it did. Lying in bed, Alma studied the details fresh in her mind that she knew so well by now. She didn't have any answers for those troubled thoughts that kept surfacing.

She pulled herself out of bed and headed toward the bathroom.

Alma paused in the doorway, a tingling sensation beckoning her. She turned slowly and stared at the empty bed.

In a flash, she saw him lying on his side, half-covered, reaching out toward her, smiling his wide, lazy smile as he tried to entice her to return to the bed—to him.

She gasped, stumbled backwards and blinked, reaching out to the wall for support. The bed WAS empty.

A frozen minute passed as she continued to stare at the queen bed, expecting him to get up and materialize in front of her. Feeling safe, she turned and fled to the bathroom, locking the door behind her.

Alma stood under the blasting shower spray and let her mind wander. Her job was hectic, the pace seldom slow. She had worked her way up in the company over the past several years starting out as a clerk in the Human Resources department.

The prestigious oil and gas service company in Houston's Galleria area was a great place to work. At one time, HR was called "Personnel." How times had changed.

She had made it to a comfortable position as employee relations supervisor at Hunter and Bloomfield and survived several oil recessions.

Besides processing applicants all day, she dealt with internal problems. Her days were long; lunches short (if any); weekends were sometimes interrupted.

The phone on her desk never had a chance to collect dust and her office door should have been replaced with a revolving turnstile.

There was never time for a private life. Her kids spent too much time in the care of other people because of her demanding job, but there was no solution. She knew if she were to find another job, after two or three months it would be the same thing all over again.

Jeff, her husband of eight years, had drowned in a boating accident two years ago at Lake Livingston, leaving her, Cody and Jamie to cope on their own. Sure, the house was paid for with the insurance money, bills had been paid off, but there was little left to subsidize her income.

At twenty-eight, she couldn't stand the contemplation of having to be the breadwinner for the rest of her life, trying to provide for her little boys. Each year the cost of food, clothing and day care increased. Paychecks didn't increase. They seemed to shrink year after year due to taxes and insurance hikes.

With the oil industry on the decline, she was lucky to have a job. Next month would mark two years since her last wage increase. She couldn't keep up with inflation. Many times, she had considered finding someone else, but had eliminated the idea right off the bat.

Step-parenting, from what she had heard from friends, was worse than a terrible marriage with the actual parent partner. Still, if there were someone else to help with raising the boys and sharing responsibilities and expenses, it would be easier.

But she would not go through all that again and end up shattered. Relationships had no guarantees attached to them, and they were an investment on heart and nerves she would rather keep wrapped up tight.

The men at work called her Miss Icicle. They used to be secretive about it, but that had changed during the past six months. She couldn't remember when; but most likely when

Doug Harris, the tall, sandy-haired, bedroom-eyed Casanova of electrical engineering called her for a lunch date. Her refusal ruffled his feathers; no one refused a date with the great lover!

He had been vicious, lashing her with his harsh words, telling her he hadn't expected the well-known *Miss Icicle* to accept because everyone knew she was challenging science and Mother Nature to recapture her virginity.

From that point on, certain men in his clique made a point of calling her the hateful name every chance they got.

Convincing herself she didn't mind, that words couldn't hurt her, she buried herself deeper in work. It bothered her though, and her boss, Ron Finkley, sensed it. He urged her to go out occasionally so she could meet a nice guy.

"You're much too young and attractive to sit and pine away for a dead man, Alma," he reminded her at least once a week. "You could be a model and make a lot more money than you'd ever earn here in a lifetime. Why don't you pursue something like that?"

He was right about the money. Anything would pay more. She still didn't have an upper-management salary but, she had the responsibility and challenge of the position, and she liked that part. Horrified at his words, she didn't agree with him about her looks.

At five-foot seven, her long auburn hair reached to her waist, and her hourglass figure had curves in all the right places. Her oval face had perfect features—prettily arched eyebrows, emerald eyes, a slender nose and full, pouting lips, high cheekbones and peaches-and-cream complexion.

But she didn't see herself in the same light that others saw her. Women were jealous of her, men dreamed about loving her, a camera lens would worship her. But she wasn't pining away for Jeff. Her boss just didn't understand that she didn't want to get hurt again.

She had accepted Jeff's death and was coping in the only way she knew. They had not been the lost-in-love couple Ron assumed they were. She and Jeff had been friends, sharing a lot, easing the loneliness in each other's lives.

If damn Doug Harris makes one cocky comment today, I'll push him down the stairs.

She turned the water off and snatched her towel.

"Cody! Jamie! Time to get up," Alma hollered down the hall as she headed to the kitchen.

Alma pressed the button on the coffee maker, found her travel cup and added one spoon of sugar and a splash of milk.

Cody wandered into the kitchen in his pajamas, holding a piece of paper. "Mom, don't forget to sign this so I can go on the field trip."

"Where are you going this time?" she asked.

"The arboretum," Cody said.

"That's right. You'll love that place. It's beautiful and peaceful," Alma said as she took a pen from the pencil cup on the counter. She signed the paper, folded it and handed it back. "Go put this in your backpack so you don't forget it. Where's your brother?"

Cody trotted out of the kitchen. "Jamie! Mom wants you!"

After the boys had dressed and ate, they headed out the door. Alma pulled up into the oak-lined horseshoe driveway to the daycare center. "Just think, after summer vacation, you will be in second grade, Jamie. And your brother will be in fifth grade!"

"When can I drive the car?" Cody asked.

Alma tried to control a belly laugh. "In about eight more years. You'll be able to see over the steering wheel and reach the brakes by then. Come on, let's get going."

They got out of the car and Alma walked them into the building and checked them in at the front desk.

Chapter 2

The white late model Chevy Impala rounded the bend not quite adhering to the thirty-five-mph speed limit.

Fondren Road north of Westheimer wound and changed names several times and never ran in a straight line. South Piney Point Road, then Blalock, then Echo Lane snaked in and out of several small exclusive Villages—separate from Houston's taxation.

As the car meandered down the street, Alma slowed to adapt to another turn. Without warning, it sputtered, then quit. Thinking quickly, she threw the gearshift into neutral, pumped the gas and tried turning the key to start it.

Nothing.

Not the clicking sound she expected to hear, or any other symptom of a dead battery.

Dead silence under the hood.

Alma swore under her breath. She remembered that the power steering wouldn't be functioning. She hit the emergency flasher button then tugged at the wheel and steered the coasting vehicle off the road, hoping it would roll far enough to get out of the way of heavy morning traffic.

Houston streets were dangerous. Speed limit signs meant nothing, except to keep people practicing their reading skills. The pace was always fast. It didn't matter that freeways had the fifty-five mph traffic signs; people raced at eighty.

Street traffic typically tripped along at fifty for the slow-pokes, speeding up to seventy, and faster on a straight stretch of road. Tires screeched at take-offs when traffic lights turned green, then again when the light flashed to red.

Most drivers seemed wary of those green lights because other drivers ran red lights. Alma didn't want to leave any room for doubt so she made sure the car rolled to the shoulder out of the way.

"Damn!" she muttered. If she had to walk back to the gas station on Westheimer, her feet would die in the taupe high heels. She wouldn't be able to leave the laptop in the car. She would have to lug the company property with her because it contained confidential information on key employees up for promotions.

That was a joke because they wouldn't get any money out of the deal, only a title change, worthless stock options, an extra week of vacation and a promise of a hefty raise *when things got better*. Oh well, H & B would survive and she had a job to do, and this laptop was her responsibility. She wouldn't take the chance just locking the car; locked cars were stolen by the dozen.

Alma pulled the hood release latch and let herself out of the car. She walked to the front of the car and pried the heavy hood up enough to gain access to the latch with her fingers.

The damn thing weighed a ton.

After several seconds, she gave up. She cussed to herself as she slammed her hands down on the hood, latching it closed. She got back into the car to stew for a few minutes and plan her next move.

Alma dug into her purse for her cellphone. She located her AAA card.

A bright red Ferrari sped past and screeched to a halt causing a chain reaction of tires screeching behind it. The driver steered to the shoulder and shifted into reverse.

The car wavered backward along the shoulder at a dangerous pace, spinning dirt and gravel with his tires, and stopped a few feet in front of Alma's car.

A jolt of shock ran through her and her jaw dropped as she recognized the tall, good-looking blond man as he got out of his car and walked toward her.

Numb, her brain froze. She couldn't come up with an explanation or any plausible answer to the questions that spun around inside her head. There was no doubt about it. This was the man she knew so intimately in her dreams.

He was real!

Mark was real!

She wanted to reach out and touch him.

"Do you need help?" he asked.

There was no mistaking the low, husky quality of his voice. It was the same as the one she heard every night.

She shivered down to her toes.

Alma didn't know if it was from fright or the sensuous memories that accompanied the voice and the sight of the man, now standing beside her car.

He leaned toward her open window.

Lest she make a fool of herself, she had to force her hands to stay clenched on the steering wheel so she didn't pull his face and lips to her.

"What seems to be the problem? Did you run out of gas?" he asked. Misinterpreting her expression, he exclaimed, "Hell, lady, I don't plan to drag you into the back seat and attack you!"

"I… I'm so sorry," she stammered, blushing. "For a minute there I thought I'd get hit by a car. When I slowed down it quit. When I shifted to neutral I may have flooded it from sheer exasperation. There's a half a tank of gas so that's not it."

"Pop the hood and I'll take a look," he said.

She thought of luxury sheets as he spoke. Alma almost moaned out loud, trembling as those white-hot memories flashed through her spinning mind.

Alma got a grasp on her singed nerves; she pulled the lever that released the heavy hood. She watched his every movement. Her eyes stuck with him as he walked to the front of the car. He lifted the white hood without effort.

Ugly words flew across her mind as she cursed the hood. She peered through the windshield between the gap in the opening of the hood from her front seat. Alma watched as he investigated the problem and checked different things.

The battery connections appeared to be in good shape. He didn't detect any loose wires. All the belts seemed intact. After several minutes, he closed the hood, then brushed his hands together. He walked back to her car door, placed his hands on the window opening and leaned forward. He looked into her eyes.

"I'm not sure what the problem is. The control module may have failed. Why don't you gather up your things and I'll take you to my place? I'm just up the street around two or three bends. I'll call a garage to come and get your car, then I'll take you to work."

About to gush an answer, she recognized the sensation as he slid inside her mind. Shocked, she stared wide-eyed into his mesmerizing blue eyes. He caressed her with those powerful hands.

She didn't have to shut her eyes. The picture was vivid. She sank under his spell, lured into the seduction as if hypnotized under a potent enchantment. Not breaking eye contact, she pulled her mind away from the powerful image.

"What are you doing? You have no right to do these things. You've been in my head for the past few weeks! Get out of my mind and stay out!" she yelled, gritting her teeth after the thrust of words.

"And don't play dumb, mister. You understand what I'm talking about. I can't figure out how you did it, but I'm positive you've disabled my car with your mind. You'd better make it right again! I am not going anywhere with you. Not now or ever. I had better not see you in my mind again!" she snapped.

She flipped hot and cold at the same instant.

He smiled coolly as he looked down at her. "I have every right in the world. I'm here to stay, Alma. You'll learn to accept it. We belong together and we will be together before long. Get used to the idea." He sauntered back to his car.

Mark stopped and turned toward her.

Even at this distance, his piercing blue eyes bore into hers.

Mark crept back into her mind and projected a provocative scene that held her captive, heart pounding. He took her face between his hands and lowered his sensuous lips to hers, rubbing them back and forth over hers, alternating between running his tongue over her lips and slipping into her mouth.

Mark claimed the response from her he wouldn't let her deny.

In the vision, she moaned with a desire to be fulfilled. Her arms wrapped around him, pulling him closer.

As she sat in the car, she succumbed to passion, weakened by the sensations. She couldn't fight him; didn't want to stop him.

As he drove off, he freed her from his sensual attack.

The feelings dissolved; her car would work again. Her fingers trembled as she grasped the keys in the ignition and started the car.

She sat behind the wheel and pulled her shattered nerves together. She forced herself to act.

Eight-twenty a.m. Late for work. How am I ever going to make it through this day? What's happening? She couldn't fathom the hold he had over her. *Him, a total stranger IN her mind!*

IN HER MIND, wholly, physically and mentally. She FELT him there. SAW him there and even WANTED him there! What possessed him to do this? What possessed her to want him never to stop?

She had a minute of clarity. That was it in a nutshell: *Possession! The devil!*

My God, maybe he's a member of one of those horrible cults I've read about online? They sacrificed animals and humans! No, that didn't sound right. Not with this sex thing! Those people would lean more towards chanting religious—or anti-religious—things. Wouldn't they?

Alma wondered what she might do about it and where to get help. If she told anyone about this, someone would take her kids away from her and lock her up in a nut house and swallow the key. There had to be an explanation.

Why me?

She shuddered. A crank caller was one thing. This was something else. She should go to the police! He must be hypnotizing and stalking her for a reason. Perhaps he was a rapist, and she might be his next victim!

She slacked off her grip on the steering wheel and flexed her fingers. She shifted into drive, activated her turn signal and eased into the traffic.

Motorists on Memorial Drive had gone berserk today, topping off the eventful morning. Alma did her best to stay accident-free, she stayed in the right-hand lane and concentrated on the road.

After a torturous three miles, she pulled into the parking lot of the seven-story office building where she worked. She thanked God she had her own parking place, or she would have been driving around in circles.

Alma gathered up her things, composed herself and headed for the front door. Nodding to the guard as she stepped inside, she didn't think she was capable of talking for fear of taking her anxieties out on him.

She waited for the slower than slow elevator which irritated her to distraction. Alma punched the button again, with vehemence, as she waited. She soon heard the mechanism going through its routine of clangs and groans as it descended to street level.

Alma hated this elevator. She dreaded the slow trip to the fifth floor, always fearing she would get trapped between floors because it wasn't a reliable mode of transportation.

At least this morning she would have things to think about during the slow trip up the five floors.

As if freed from a cage, she bolted through the doors when they opened. Alma hated being late, something that rarely happened. She was always the first person in the building, except for the security guard.

She veered left, past the area where applicants were first seen and greeted by Janet, the receptionist. With a pasted smile on her face, Alma nodded to the woman then entered through a door marked "private."

She hurried down the short corridor to her locked office.

Alma fumbled in her purse for her keys, then groped for the correct key. She almost dropped the laptop. She balanced everything and unlocked the door, walked over to her desk and dumped her keys, the laptop and her purse.

She abruptly flopped down in her chair, her legs sprawled out in front of her, and hung her arms over the arms of the chair.

Alma leaned her head back and closed her eyes. Boy, did she feel wiped out! Wasn't it time to go home yet, she wondered?

Molly, her cheerful young assistant, smiled brightly as she bounced into the room full of exuberant energy.

"Good grief, Ms. Weston, you sure look like you had a bad night! Are you all right?" the bubbly nineteen-year-old asked.

After working at the firm through two summer intern programs, Alma had hired Molly right out of high school and the young woman still called her Ms. Weston. She had given up on trying to get past the formal barrier.

From an old-world family, Molly was taught to respect her elders, and she always addressed Alma "properly."

"Can I get you a cup of coffee?" Molly asked.

"That would be nice. I've had a bad start this morning and I can use all the help I can get," Alma said.

"Are Cody and Jamie giving you a hard time, Ms. Weston?"

"No. I had car trouble just as I reached the bend at Piney Point. Typical insane traffic. I thought I'd cause an accident before I got the damn car off the road. Why haven't they widened that road?" Alma ranted.

"Did you have to get your car towed?" Molly asked.

She winced at the memory. "No, a man stopped and helped me."

"Well, that sure was nice of him," Molly said.

Alma harrumphed.

"My dad always tells me to wait for a cop to stop if I break down, but that's ridiculous. I'd end up waiting forever. You can't ever find one when you need one. Dad says not to take help from strangers. He thinks everyone is a murderer or a rapist," Molly said.

"It's wise to be cautious," Alma said.

"I should call him and tell him about your experience. Maybe he'll change his attitude. Well, I'll get you a nice cup of coffee; you need a caffeine boost after your bad start," Molly said as she left Alma's office.

She shook her head as Molly left. Alma reflected on the total experience.

I don't think it's a good idea to tell your dad my story. If he had all the details, he'd make you quit your job this instant and pack you off to a convent. Alma doubted anyone would believe this even if she had proof!

Okay, time to get started.

She dumped her purse in the bottom drawer of her desk, then turned to the laptop, docked it and booted it up. She sifted through the files of the employees to make sure they were all there, then created an email to the managers to review them. In minutes, the email was complete, along with the attached employee files.

Molly returned with a cup of coffee in one hand and a white, oblong florist box in the other hand.

"Someone's sent you flowers!" the girl exclaimed.

Alma never received personal mail, rarely received personal phone calls unless one of the boys became ill, and never flowers!

"What?" She stared at Molly as if she made a mistake. "For me? Are you sure? Who in the world…" she stopped in mid-sentence and stared at the box as if it held a decomposed body part. She thought about the potential sender.

Molly set the long box on Alma's desk and waited for her to open it.

With mixed emotions, Alma lifted the white cover and folded back the green florist paper, exposing more than a dozen deep red roses.

An envelope lay across the long, thorn-free stems. She somehow recognized the bold handwriting.

How could I recognize his handwriting?

With fingers trembling, she withdrew the card. "You have no cause to fear me," she read. "Have dinner with me? We need to talk."

How dare he! No cause? Does he think I'm a simpleton? How could you not fear someone who appeared IN your mind? That's not even a healthy thought!

He made her mental competency a major issue as far as she was concerned. If the story were to get out, she'd be declared nuts, hands down and hauled off to the nearest insane asylum!

Furious to the point of becoming borderline irrational, she crammed the tissue paper on top of the delicate red petals and looked up to see Molly's horrified expression.

Even more furious than before, because Molly didn't understand the reason behind her anger, Alma slammed the cover on the box. Then, having second thoughts, she lifted the lid, retrieved the card and tore the card into tiny pieces.

When she was satisfied with the level of destruction, she lifted the cover and dumped the mess into the middle of the tissue paper, then slammed the lid shut, denting the white box.

"Molly, please take these unwanted flowers and get rid of them," she said to the shocked assistant, determined not to give any explanation. No one would understand anyway, so it would be best to keep quiet.

"Ms. Weston! I can't believe it! Are you sure?"

"Yes Molly, I am sure. Just get rid of them for me, will you? You can even stuff them in the shredder if you'd like."

"I guess I'll give them back to the driver. I was so excited I forgot to tell you he was waiting for a reply to the note," Molly sputtered.

Her boss was the most rational person she ever worked for, and this behavior was most unusual.

She wondered who sent the beautiful roses, but obviously they weren't from someone she cared about! Her boss didn't have a boyfriend as far as she recalled; Molly didn't think Alma even dated.

If it hadn't been for the uniformed driver, Molly would have suspected Doug Harris, but he would not go to the expense of hiring someone as decked out as this driver just to deliver roses to Alma. He seemed to be the type to stop at the grocery store and cheap out.

Alma tugged a blank sheet of paper from the printer, then grabbed a big fat black marker. She wrote GO TO HELL, folded the paper, words up, and shoved it on top of the roses.

Molly blinked. Her head spun from glimpsing this odd side of her boss. She picked up the box, turned and walked out the door without uttering a word.

A look of surprise crossed the chauffeur's brown face as he waited, hands clasped behind his back, holding his hat. The look vanished, replaced with a professional, impersonal expression.

Molly handed over the long, dented white box into the groomed, brown hands.

"I'm sorry, but my boss said she can't accept the flowers." She squirmed, uncomfortable with this personal task.

The driver shifted the box into the crook of one arm, lifted his hat to his head, bowed slightly, then turned on his heels and walked out the door, never saying a word.

Molly hurried to the window, waited, and glimpsed the man getting into a sleek, silver Rolls Royce parked below the window. She wished they had been her flowers!

Mystified, Alma sat at her desk. A thousand feelings whirled through her mind.

How did that damn man know where she worked?

She pushed her chair back as she got to her feet, crossed the floor and closed her door. She wanted to be alone to rest her mind. Alma sat down and propped her elbows on her desk and hid her face in her hands.

Why me! I invited none of this.

The room was quiet as she leaned back in her chair, resting her head against the padded back. She closed her eyes and tried to clear her thoughts so she could work. She needed a fresh start to get her through the day; there would be no working late tonight, she vowed.

He caught her off-guard. He slipped into her mind quickly, attacking her senses by kissing and caressing her, filling her with wanton passion.

As she envisioned them together, him passionate with his lovemaking, her consumed with a desire so strong she shook.

She was shocked by the realization she had no control over her thoughts. He filled every corner of her mind while her physical body tingled with his every touch.

What happened inside her mind was felt on her conscious body and her mind had no control over it.

While she was locked inside this mind play, an eerie scene flashed through her brain—stalagmite-like mountains, red rocky terrain, a grey-blue sky with four hazy moons hanging in balance along the horizon.

Fantastic pewter-colored buildings in the shape of domes upon domes, and tall dark steel blue pyramid spikes dotted the landscape. She didn't see any vehicles, people or animals in the scene, yet Alma sensed they were there.

The scene vanished as suddenly as it had appeared, taking its memory with it, burying itself deep within the archives of her mind.

Released from the mesmerized state, she had a difficult time sifting through all the jumbled forced experiences of the mysterious man from her mind. Alma ached in places she assumed had died long ago.

She tried quelling the feelings that battled to come alive once more.

Was she so lonely that she fantasized this man into real life? A psychiatrist would have a field day with her *problem*. The feelings she had were real, the sexual experience was not of her own making.

How could the mental images produce physical sensations? A person would have to be sick to make these things up.

Not needing birth control pills at this point in her life, she wondered if, JUST IF, it was possible for her to become pregnant?

God Almighty!

What would she do? Alma shook her head and closed her eyes. It had been a rotten day from the beginning.

The number one priority for the day was to go online to the public library and search for some books to help her with this situation. She was sure the branch near H & B would have what she wanted. If not, she would request them from a different branch. If her library branch had what she wanted, she would stop on the way home since tonight was the only night it stayed open late.

She discovered her library had two books she wanted to read. She requested them so they would be at the front desk when she got off work. Alma picked up her pen to make notations on a pad, pondering over a job description she tried to write. Her eyes glided across the room to the door.

In a flash, an image popped up: The jean-clad man leaned against the door, smiling at her. She jumped up, thrust her chair backward and sucked in her breath, eyes wild, ready to shriek.

As quickly as the image had appeared, it vanished, leaving her heart pounding and her mouth hanging open. She groped for her chair, eased down into it and stared at the door.

Alma sat quietly pondering all the events. Daydreaming seemed to be the key. When she spaced out, he slid inside her mind. She would have to figure out how to stop daydreaming. That seemed like her only defense.

"Thank you very much, Mrs. Moore. I love being able to go online and have books waiting for me," Alma told the tiny, yellow haired librarian.

"If they don't work out for you, dear, just return them. If there are others at another branch, we can always request them for you. It only takes a few days to get something transferred from one branch to another unless they're checked out," the kind librarian said.

Alma left the library and drove to the daycare center. The boys would be surprised to see her picking them up on time. This daycare offered extended stay services for an additional fee.

The daycare center where they stayed after school was a nice place, but not home. It got noisy during the afternoon when the children had free play; otherwise it provided a structured environment with fun things to do and parents considered it one of the better facilities on her side of town.

The little blue van took her two sons to school, picked them up in the afternoon and brought them back to the day-care center where they had a snack, watched a children's educational show on Netflix, or took part in a planned activity.

And was it expensive! One hundred sixty-five dollars a week for before and after school each day, per child! When she added the extended stay fee she shuddered.

Thinking of the money she used to pay when the boys were toddlers, she knew she could never afford that now. It was almost impossible to come out ahead when you had more than one child.

When Jeff had been alive, he had made good money as a programmer, so it had been reasonable for her to pursue a career. Back then she enjoyed it. Her paycheck was used for savings and extra fun things.

That was all in the past. Now, it was a necessity, drudgery. Some days worse than others. Resentment filled her from her toes to her forehead.

Those dangerous days hung in a fine balance where she fought emotions tugging her in nine million directions.

QUIT YOUR JOB her brain would scream, trying to convince her that a job operating a cash register at Walmart would solve all her problems. Since that wasn't practical and wouldn't support her and the boys, she continued to get up each morning and go through the ritual of getting ready for work.

As she pulled into the driveway of the daycare center, she glimpsed her two boys through the glass walls. A lot of the kids watched the cars pull up in front of the building in the afternoon, waiting for their parents to pick them up, ready to go home and be a part of a family.

As she watched, they waved their hands at her one minute then scattered in different directions, gathering up their belongings the next.

Within minutes, a helper escorted Cody and Jamie out to the car amid the screams of "hi mom", and settled them into their belt positioning booster seats, then locked the door.

"Hi boys! Are you both settled into your seats? Did you have a nice day today? Tell me what you learned," she said.

"Mom! You'll never guess what! Jason's mother is P-R-E-G-N-A-N-T." Cody carefully spelled out the word.

"What's that?" Jamie asked, wide-eyed.

"Oh, the word Cody spelled is pregnant, Jamie. Your brother means that Mrs. Summers is going to have a baby," Alma explained to her younger son.

"Mom! Don't tell Jamie that! He's too young to know about that stuff!" Cody squealed horrified.

"Cody, your brother is not too young to know about that stuff! You were way younger than Cody when I was PREG-NANT, remember? Was I supposed to hide from you because of my condition?

"You're only two years older than your brother and he's not a baby, so stop treating him like one, for heaven's sake!" Her eight-year-old acted like forty sometimes.

"Can we go to Chick-fil-A, Mom?" Jamie pleaded.

"Sure, why not? A milk shake should tide you over until I can get supper fixed. Do you want peppermint chocolate, Cody?"

"Yeah!"

"Cookies and cream, Jamie?"

Jamie scrunched up his face. "Strawberry!"

"Are you sure?" Alma asked. "Once you order, it's yours."

"Today's a strawberry day," Jamie said.

"Okay." Alma pulled up to the order window.

After getting supper behind them and cleaning up the dirty dishes, Alma relaxed in her preferred spot stretched out on the three-cushioned, old blue corduroy sofa.

She leaned her head back and closed her eyes. She shut out the TV as the boys watched their favorite show on Netflix, *Ask the StoryBots*. Jamie and Cody loved the show, along with *Project Mc2*. Alma allowed them to stay up past their usual bedtime to watch one episode. Ordinarily, Jamie was in bed by eight, and Cody followed at eight-thirty.

The show ended, and the boys turned off the TV. The house was blessed with quiet as the boys went to their bedrooms to settle down for the night. After a few minutes, Alma went down the hallway, tucked them in bed and kissed them goodnight. She returned to the sofa and sank down into the blue cushions.

Alma had brought nothing home from work.

That's my rebellious side roaring.

She settled down with one of the library books. She scanned through the table of contents, then flipped to the index.

Not what I expected. I'll return it tomorrow.

She reached for the second book.

This was supposed to be about the inner powers of the mind. She browsed through it but couldn't quite tell if it was just about meditation, or if it went deeper, but she read the first chapter, and decided to see what else the book contained. After five pages, she resolved to read the whole thing.

Chapter two instructed Alma about concentrating on something so intently that she could block everything else out of her mind. After several minutes of serious considerations, she chose the ocean—waves caressing the beach in serene peacefulness, a full moon shining golden across the peaks of water.

She leaned back with eyes closed and pictured the lapping waves and erased other troubles and pictures from her mind. It was difficult at first; everyday things crept into the peace and shattered the picture, forcing her to begin again. The chattering was non-stop and loud; she would have to practice every day.

Concentrate. Concentrate. With her eyes closed, scenes flashed across the black void of screen on her eyelids.

In a split second, a dozen good choices zapped in front of her and left.

Fully aware of the importance of this task, she concentrated on finding an object, but what could she choose to train her mind?

The waves would not work, their lapping was distracting, the scene way too busy; she needed a mental weapon against Mark. Something strong. Something sure.

She would fight his intrusions and win.

Chapter 3

A lma glanced at the clock in the kitchen, yawned and stretched.

She pulled herself up from the comfortable sofa and walked across the living room to the master bedroom, flicking off lights and locking up. Alma stopped for a quick look at the thermostat to adjust the dial for a comfortable night.

Waking up like a popsicle from the air conditioning didn't rate a happy thought. She continued to the kitchen and locked the back door, turned off that light, then returned to her bedroom.

After pulling off her clothes, she discarded each item in the wicker hamper in her garden bathroom.

Bedecked with bountiful hanging plants, the room was the determining factor in buying the house. Along with the two shell-shaped cream-colored sinks in the vanity, the private toilet area, his and hers huge walk-in closets, a tub and a stall shower—nothing would budge her decision and Jeff had known it.

After slipping a green, silky nightie over her head, she stretched and yawned.

Ah, the wonders of fake silk! Real silk is ten times better, but I can't splurge on that.

Alma did her usual routine and climbed into bed. She picked up her library book and scooted across the bed on her knees until she was almost in the middle. Stretched out on her stomach with the book in front of her, she resumed reading.

After ten minutes of the intense reading, her eyes got heavy. She closed the book, switched off the lamp and drifted into sleep. Her last conscious thought was of Mark.

Damn! This mind-control business will take work!

Hard at work, Alma's mind searched for something. An image to use as a weapon. Her mind flitted from one idea to another, continuing its search. Crossed swords. A serpent. Many things swept through her mind.

The search halted, pushed aside by an intruder.

"You are learning quickly. Your mind is a powerful tool, but you aren't aware of that yet, are you, Alma? More powerful than Asedi. He's very jealous and will send others to hunt you.

"There is no time to spare for games; you have much to learn. The dormant side of your brain must awaken soon for you to survive.

"Our marriage must take place. Our children need protecting. Sleep tonight, my love."

He kissed her sleeping lips. He exited, leaving Alma to sleep peacefully.

Alma woke fifteen minutes before the alarm sounded. She lay in a half-asleep state, trying to recall her dreams.

Positive, then doubtful, she remembered talking to someone.

No; someone had talked to her.

There were no memories of passion, no blue eyes. No strong, masculine body being molded to hers in the heat of passion.

How disappointing.

She missed him, missed his nearness, missed his lovemaking.

Loneliness engulfed her. She wanted to wail—she weighed the emptiness and hated it. One minute she loved him; the next she hated him for his invasion.

BBUUUZZZZ!

Alma flinched awake and rolled over and slammed her hand on the snooze button. Her heart pounded as feelings surfaced and she remembered she had wakened earlier, but she must have dozed off again. She felt down this morning and didn't understand why.

She remembered the crossed swords. Alma closed her eyes and envisioned the pair of gleaming weapons.

It was difficult to keep little things out of her mind. Tennis shoes, breakfast dishes, work files, all crowded in for attention.

She pushed each item out of the way and returned her concentration to the main focal point: a pair of crossed swords.

Junk kept sneaking in. Concentration was difficult. She would do it, eventually. It would take more effort on her part. She would not give up.

The buzzer sounded again. This time she shut off the alarm. She bounded out of bed and headed toward the bathroom and a nice hot morning shower to scrub all the ghosts away. She felt alert, rested and refreshed as she donned her robe and headed toward the kitchen.

Each day began the same way: juice for three, toast—one with butter, one with strawberry jam, one with grape jelly. Cereal—two bowls of Cheerios, one bowl of mini shredded wheat; regular milk, none of that watery low-fat milk for her family.

She walked down the hall and stopped at Jamie's room first. He was sprawled on his stomach, mouth hanging open, soaking a corner of his pillow, limbs askew. She rubbed his back and called to him softly.

"Time to wake up, sleepy head. Come on, Jamie, that's enough sleep for one night. Up and at 'em!"

Alma opened the closet door and chose a pair of jeans, then dug in the dresser for the rest of his clothes and laid them all at the foot of his bed.

"Jamie, your clothes are ready. If you don't like the shirt I picked out, find something else to wear. Come on now, we're on a schedule."

She left Jamie, she went to wake Cody, across the hall. He was just beginning to stir, stretching the remnants of sleep out of his stiff limbs.

"Hi, Mom," the towhead said. "Did I beat you this morning?"

"You sure did. Before long, I'll be able to use you for an alarm clock. Do you want me to get your clothes ready or do you want to pick them out today?"

"Can I wear my Sponge Bob shirt today, mom?" he asked.

"It's a little too tight for you, Cody. I think you should give it to your brother."

"Aw, Mom!" he protested. He screwed his face into a look of rebellion.

"Don't argue about clothes. Just get dressed." He was getting very picky with his wardrobe.

Alma left the boys to get dressed. She returned to her bedroom and studied the clothes in her closet. She chose a full-skirted dress with small blue, rust, and tan flowers on a white background. The colors complimented her hair and skin, and it was one of her favorite things to wear.

Alma took the soft cotton and polyester dress off the hanger and laid it on the bed. She searched for her navy pumps in the shoe rack next, then located the navy plastic belt and snatched her blue faux leather purse off the top shelf in the closet.

She swapped the contents from the purse she had used the day before.

A shrewd shopper, she always chased after sales. Not being able to afford the better stores didn't bother her very much; she located nice-looking clothes at less expensive shops, found purses in every color priced under twenty dollars, and matched shoes to her finds from a discount shoe store.

The boys' wardrobes were put together with the same care. Discount stores were clothes heaven for young boys' clothes. They were abundant; the sizes and styles were in vogue with what other boys were wearing, except for the extreme styles, and she could budget their summer, winter, and school clothes at most places.

Everyone ended up happy with the choices, but she knew when the boys got older, they would not want to continue shopping at discount stores. Cody was already rebelling, and she hated even thinking of the next school year. It would be a challenge to dress that kid.

The morning routine was well under way; clothes donned, breakfast eaten, dishes rinsed and placed in the dishwasher. Alma shooed the boys out to the car.

They buckled-up into their car seats with some grumbles between them, but everyone settled in for the ride. Thank God school would be out for the summer in three weeks. The temperature was already sizzling.

They arrived at the daycare center, and Alma made sure Cody and Jamie had lunch money, then kissed them goodbye before they left the car. She had given up making lunches long ago, discovering it was easier and cheaper to buy hot lunches at school.

She had gotten tired of running to the school with a replacement lunch if one of the boys lost their bag or left it at the daycare center.

Alma watched them walk to the front door of the center and reflected about how big they were getting. When they were safely inside, she steered the car toward the busy road to continue toward work.

"Morning, Ms. Weston," said John, the security guard. He reminded her of a nice Southern gentleman, always polite, complimentary and friendly. He started her days off right.

"My, you sure look pretty today. Have a nice day."

"Why, thank you, John. Don't you work too hard either! Oh, and before I forget, next Sunday, we're running an ad in the *Chronicle* for two positions, so I imagine we'll have people coming in for interviews.

"I'll give you a list of applicants each day, but I'm sure we'll have our share of drop-ins. I'll also make sure that Molly gives you a supply of application forms and pens so you'll be prepared," she said to the silver-haired guard.

The cranky elevator made its regular trip to her floor, stopped and hesitated several seconds before opening its doors.

Alma had an uneasy thought that today was the day she would become trapped inside. Her nerves jerked when the doors only opened about three inches. They paused, then slid the rest of the way open. This old elevator was getting worse every week.

She would have Molly call the elevator company to come out and see what they could do with it.

A conscientious person, Alma liked getting to work early and being prepared, not waiting until the last minute to organize items in a rush.

When she arrived at seven thirty, there was enough time to get files in order on her desk, study her calendar for appointments, write memos for Molly to distribute, and drink a peaceful cup of coffee before her phone began the never-ending ringing.

There were also special occasions when she came in early to interview individuals who could not come to the office during normal business hours.

Around seven-fifty, people arrived in groups. Several employees stopped, one by one, to offer their morning greetings.

Evelyn, one of the young admins, poked her head through the open doorway of Alma's office. "I've got a problem, and I'd like to meet with you before you get bogged down with interviews."

Familiar with Evelyn's dilemma, Alma suspected she could guess what the problem was and gave her an appointment for eight-thirty. That should give Evelyn enough time to get her boss settled.

Situations rolled through her mind and she sympathized with Evelyn. The woman had a good background of experience, a level head on her shoulders, and always did a quality job. The problem was her boss, Lance Taylor. Southern gentleman he was not.

Why do we still employ this lecherous cad? He's not even that good looking yet acts as though a line of wanton women are waiting to break his door down. I don't know what to do about him.

He border-lined getting into trouble with the Equal Employment Opportunity Commission, Title 7, for sexual harassment.

All in a day's work.

She shook her head. At least her job was not boring. The situations varied with each employee and applicant. The different people she worked with at employment agencies added extra flavor to her workday.

They're always trying to sell their applicants to the highest bidder.

Some candidates turned out to be a good match, but quite a few were undesirable.

In the past, she had dealt with two agencies that had given her a hard time. The overbearing go-between at the agency would send unqualified people to see her, wasting both her and the candidate's time.

She figured out what was going on—they had to satisfy two objectives: send a warm body to see the important client and send the candidate out so he thinks you're working hard to place him.

That didn't fly with Alma; her day was too hectic to waste time with someone who didn't fit the criteria.

She finally took matters into her own hands by going over the agency contact's head—in both cases, by going directly to the owner of the firm.

The problem was cleared immediately, and she never heard from either of the offending people after that. She now got her best applicants from those two agencies.

Eight-thirty rolled around. The phone buzzed and Molly announced that Evelyn had arrived. She promptly escorted her in.

"Hi, Evelyn. What can I do for you today?" Alma said.

"Alma, I'm giving Lance my two-week notice Friday. I wanted to tell you first because you've done so much for me. Honestly, I don't know what you will do about filling this position. I'd hate to see a young, innocent woman take my place because I don't think it would be fair to her. I'm surprised Mrs. Taylor hasn't divorced him by now. Surely she sees the way he goes after women."

"I had suspected you wouldn't stay, and I can't blame you. Please give my name as the person to contact for a reference, and I'll see you get standing ovations!" Alma ignored her comments about Mrs. Taylor.

I don't understand why we don't fire that slimy bastard.

"I hate to leave, but it's time I moved on, anyway. I've been here three years, and there isn't a whole lot more that I can learn," Evelyn said.

"That's understandable. Good luck, Evelyn. You won't have any trouble at all finding something that suits you." Alma stood. The two women shook hands, then Evelyn left.

Alma sat back down and woke her computer. She typed a note in Evelyn's file, then jotted a note on her desk calendar. She tapped her pen on the desk and contemplated about the situation with the engineer.

Better talk to the boss about this. It's time to decide what to do about Lance. The man either has to be warned or put on probation. The company can't afford a sexual harassment suit, or the bad publicity. Should throw in the prob-

lem with Doug Harris as well. He needs to be taken down a peg or two.

She sighed in exasperation. Alma cleared the matter out of her mind. Her first interview, Jack Braden, was at ten-thirty.

The mechanical engineer had an impressive resume, and she hoped that he interviewed well because they needed to fill that spot.

Alma went through the standard procedures and talked to the candidate for fifteen minutes giving him generic information about the position which had been glossed over in the online ad.

They discussed the strength of the company in the not too steady environment and she outlined the reasons Hunter and Bloomfield was not affected by the present oil industry gloom.

After she completed her standard presentation, she escorted him to Fred Bailey, one of three managers who would interview the prospective employee. Braden had interviewed well with her and Alma was sure he would get the job.

"Fred, this is Jack Braden. Jack, Fred has been with Hunter and Bloomfield for fifteen years," Alma said. "I'll see you after your interviews, Jack."

The salary Hunter and Bloomfield planned to offer him was more than what he was making, and the benefits were outstanding—enough to entice someone away from their present employer.

He still had to go through the circuit of department interviews, but she seemed confident that the three most important people he needed to see would feel as she did. He was what they were looking for.

Molly interrupted her daydreaming. She approached the desk as if something urgent needed attention.

Alma noticed the high color on her cheeks.

"Ms. Weston, a Mr. St. Claire is here to see you and I don't have his name on the list of people you're supposed to see today. God, what a dreamboat!" Molly emphasized, rolling her eyes. "Do you want me to send him in?"

Scanning the list of names on her calendar, Alma picked up the yellow-lined tablet she used to make notes on. No St. Claire.

"Molly, did he say what he was here for? Is he looking for a job?" Alma asked. "He's not on either of my lists."

"Oops, I forgot to ask! He's so good looking I got tongue-tied. I'm sorry, Ms. Weston. Let me go find out what he wants." Molly left the room, embarrassed.

Smiling, Alma shook her head. Molly was very impressionable. Turning to Jack Braden's file folder, she made notations on one of the standard forms. Silently, like a fog rolling across damp ground, an image entered her mind.

Tell Molly you forgot all about our appointment, Alma. We'll stay for a few minutes, then we'll go to lunch.

Mark's image vanished, leaving her shaking.

Within minutes, Molly came back into the room. "He said he was an old friend, Ms. Weston, and that you probably forgot about your lunch date!"

"How could I have forgotten! It's been so long since I heard his last name." Alma spoke in a rush, hoping to convince Molly with the lie. "Show him in."

Molly narrowed her eyes as she left the room.

Why is my boss behaving so strangely? Maybe it's because this is her first date since her husband died?

Minutes later Mark stood in the doorway, a vision of elegance and sophistication in a dark blue Armani suit, pale blue shirt and red-flecked tie. His blue eyes captured hers. He seemed to fill the room with his presence.

He shut the door and crossed the floor to sit in the chair in front of her desk, crossing one leg over the other.

Alma felt awkward. She said nothing. She sat there and returned his stare.

Mesmerized, she couldn't have broken the eye contact if she wanted to.

He held her captive. She didn't feel him or see him in her mind, but she felt whisper kisses against her skin, making her nipples harden.

"Shall we get used to each other's voices?" His was as smooth as satin.

Too shocked to answer, Alma nodded.

"We have a lot to talk about. There are things you should know. Things you won't believe or understand. It is unavoidable, and can't be put off any longer," he said.

Waiting for him to continue, she sat spellbound. All she could think about were his eyes.

Those irresistible blue, blue eyes. When they looked at her...

"Nothing to say?" he asked, smiling.

Alma came out of her stupor. "What could we possibly have in common to talk about? You're a damn pervert, you know that? You're just like a peeping Tom the way you intrude upon my privacy."

Her eyes blazed with anger and her cheeks turned pink.

"The things we have in common will shock you." He leaned forward in his chair. His eyes softened as he continued to gaze at her. "Come on, let's go. We've played this game long enough."

"Wh-where are we going?" she asked, stuttering after a minute's silence, feeling stupid for the lack of an intelligent question.

"I thought you might like to see where I live," he replied playfully. "You didn't want to yesterday, remember?"

Stiffening, Alma already knew one room in that house although she made no reference to it now.

"Shall we go?"

"I'll agree to this onetime event, but don't think this is going to become a habit." Alma gathered her purse. She rolled her chair back and made room to stand.

Alma walked around the desk which had been a safe barrier between them. It was agonizing as she felt him watching her movements. She felt vulnerable and quickened her pace to reach the door.

Mark reached out and grasped her wrist, causing her to cry out in fright.

As if turned to stone, Alma stopped.

Physical contact with him was unbearable.

Scenes raced through her mind and, unknown to her, he read them.

He tugged her arm. Mark moved to face Alma. He moved one hand up her arm, sensuously stroking her soft skin while placing his other hand on her waist; he drew her to him.

When his lips lowered to hers, she knew what to expect.

Explosions of sensuality.

She burned with almost uncontrolled passion racing through her body. Her arms went around his neck of their own accord, demanding.

Her hands found their familiar place in his hair. Hunger consumed her, passion fueled her.

She wanted to climb onto his body.

When the kiss ended, he whispered.

"It will never change between us, no matter how hard you try to fight me. Do you understand, Alma?"

Ready to bolt like a trapped animal, she stared at him, fear stretching across her face.

"What in the hell kind of hold do you have over me?" she asked, loudly, pushing him away.

"For two weeks you've tormented me at night, then you appear in my life as if nothing is wrong! I'm a simple person. I've done nothing out of the ordinary in my entire life. I never cheated on my husband, I don't beat my kids, but I feel as though you're trying to drag me to the depths of Hell. Why?"

Mark crept inside her mind and commanded her to reach a calm, reasonable state. He took hold of her hand and placed it on his arm.

"We'll discuss the matter after we leave your office."

As he pulled on the door, he nodded to show that she should precede him.

She slipped out of his hold and walked coolly into the outer room.

"Molly, we're leaving for lunch."

Embarrassed, Alma was sure Molly had overheard her yelling at Mark, but she decided not to make an issue of it.

"She may be back late," Mark told Molly, winking.

Nodding dumbly, Molly stared after the couple.

As if Mark controlled such things, the elevator responded immediately to his call.

Dumbfounded, Alma could not believe the thing didn't take the usual lengthy amount of time to reach the fifth floor.

The doors opened silently, and they stepped inside.

Mark pushed the ground floor button then turned toward Alma.

"Concentrate on Kredo," he ordered, seriously.

"What?" She looked at him as if he were demented. "Am I supposed to know what that means? Is it a thing or a place or a person?"

Her brows furrowed.

A vision flashed past in her mind.

She remembered something, beyond her reach, but she couldn't quite focus on the memory.

She placed her hand on her forehead and closed her eyes tightly as if forcing the memory to return.

Something passed behind her closed eyelids, but she couldn't grasp it.

Holding her face tenderly in his hands, he whispered one word: *Remember*.

The elevator reached the ground floor; the door opened smoothly. They stepped out into the bright lobby of the glass and concrete building. The sleek silver car was waiting at the curb. Opening the back door, Marked helped Alma inside, then got in himself and closed the door.

"Home, Preston," he said to the uniformed man behind the wheel.

Preston nodded.

Chapter 4

Hidden in the massive, dense, wooded area off the main road was a private, paved, winding driveway. Only someone familiar with the property would find it with ease while driving by on the main road.

Preston guided the quiet car down a beautiful, tree-lined drive. Sunshine drifted down through the trees, giving the appearance of a settling fog.

Nestled in a well thought out planned clearing stood the house.

Alma gasped with surprise when she saw the structure at the end of the long drive. What Mark called home looked more like a fortress.

Surrounded by a high brick wall, the twenty-room mansion demanded attention, beautiful in its old-world design. It looked like something from an English countryside; it seemed so authentic.

"How beautiful! It looks like a castle. How lucky for you to live in such a wonderful house!" For the minute she forgot her former feelings for the man—a mixture of fright and want.

"I'm happy you like it, Alma. It has all the modern conveniences. My home is your home," he said, leaving her confused.

He placed Alma's hand on his arm and covered it with his, then led her up the wide, stone stairs.

The front door swung open and Alma saw a dignified man in a formal butler's uniform standing back to allow them to pass. The butler stood ramrod-straight, a picture of efficiency in his fitted clothing.

"Good morning, Spencer," Mark greeted the man. "We have a guest for lunch. Alma, this is Spencer. He sees to everything."

"A pleasure, Miss Alma." The proper man bowed. "If you'll excuse me, I'll make sure Cook has everything ready." He glided away.

The interior of the house sprawled with spacious high ceilings and elaborate crown moldings.

Alma's eyes wandered from the oriental rugs and tapestries to the elegant antique furniture, chandeliers, and gleaming wood floors.

As Mark toured Alma through the rooms, giving her a brief history of the furnishings, she stopped to get a closer look at certain items. She wouldn't touch or pick up anything fearing that she would break something precious.

The rooms looked like pages out of a decorating book. She daydreamed the way these house furnishings would compare to the great homes in England.

They climbed the wide, polished stairs to the second floor. Each guest suite had a private sitting room, bathroom, and an elegant bedroom, he told her.

Pastel colors brightened each theme. The second floor included an informal gathering room where guests congregated before retiring to their own sitting rooms.

Mark guided Alma down a hallway lined with pictures in gilded frames. Paintings of landscapes, portraits, and some animals. She recognized names of famous artists on several paintings. She guessed that the others most likely equaled in value, but not being very knowledgeable about art, she couldn't be sure.

They reached the end of the long gallery hall. Mark turned to the door on the right.

Alma stiffened. She didn't need a guide to describe this room. Mark opened the door and stood back for her to enter first. She hesitated, her eyes raking the room, then walked through the opening.

The sitting room appeared masculine, but not overpowering, with a desk and chair, a brown leather sofa, two wingback chairs, end tables, and other small items. Another doorway revealed a dressing room. Beyond that the master bedroom.

Yes. She would recognize this room anywhere.

The room walked right out of her dreams; the high spindle bed, the other furniture, everything down to the last detail. As pictures flashed through her mind, Alma's eyes froze on the vast bed.

The memories of the room overpowered her. Underneath the cream-colored covering, white luxury cotton sheets, so soft and smooth, called to her.

If she closed her eyes her body would recall those cool sheets against her skin along with Mark's imprint in the middle of the bed. She shuddered.

"And this is my room," Mark said, ending the tour.

Startled, she jumped as his seductive voice broke through the quiet of the room.

Turning to face him, she stared into his eyes, seeking something.

"Yes, I'm aware that this is your room. I want answers! Have you been hypnotizing me into believing I have been here before? How have you done these things?"

"Suggestions and sensory thoughts, my dear," he answered.

"You're lying." She swung around, breaking eye contact with him. As her eyes inspected the room, she noticed one of the framed pictures on a side table.

A memory stirred in her mind, too deep to surface. The handsome couple seemed familiar to her, but their names alluded her. Their clothing appeared unusual, but not from another century.

She tried to pull the origins from her memories but failed.

"Hester." Alma whispered the woman's name, scrunched her eyes closed, and placed her fingertips to her temples.

The man's name wouldn't surface. It remained a mystery to her, buried deep within a trap inside her mind.

Pictures of two families flashed past like lightning. The name still eluded her.

"My parents," Mark said. "Hester and Nalzen at Tarden House." He watched Alma for a response to the information—a critical memory that needed to resurface.

"Tarden House. Is that in England? Why does that name seem familiar? Have I ever been there?" she asked, brows furrowed.

"No, it's not in England; it's in Cralic Sector. You lived there a long time ago, when you were a child. My parents adored you from the moment of your birth."

"Cralic Sector. Cralic Sector. Why does that place sound so familiar? What a strange name," she said. "Where is that? I can't seem to remember."

"Very far away. Your guardians moved you here to raise you away from your home world." He planted pieces of information for her to think about.

"Home world? What does that even mean? Are you demented? I've lived here all my life, first with my parents, then with Aunt Rose and Uncle Donald after my parents died," she said.

"We lived a very sedate life. We never did anything out of the ordinary, and we never traveled. We even stayed home during the summer. I am positive I never went to Tarden House with them."

"Our families are more than close friends. I birthed six years before you. When you came along, a picture-perfect green-eyed little girl, our parents arranged our betrothal," he stated.

"You remember my mother; the memory is there. How she loved you. Our mothers spent hours planning every detail of our wedding."

"Betrothal? Wedding? You're crazy! My parents would never do anything like that!" Alma felt threatened and confused.

She stepped back from the dangerous, unbalanced man before her.

"You wouldn't even recognize your parents if they stood in front of you! How can you even try to guess their decisions? You and I are both the only children of our families and our parents wanted to bind the families together in marriage."

"This isn't medieval times, for Christ's sake! I come from right here in Houston. My parents were normal everyday modern people. You're sick!" she ranted. She distanced herself from him.

"Do you remember your parents, Alma? Have you ever seen pictures of them? The answer is NO! The people who raised you were not relatives. They were guardians appointed by your parents to bring you here and care for you until the revolution ended," he explained, with force.

"Revolution? What revolution are you talking about? What country? My parents died in a car accident before my first birthday! How could I possibly remember them?" she protested. "No infant has memories of their life at that age?"

"Can you explain why your 'aunt' and 'uncle' didn't display any pictures of your parents or their home? All families have pictures, whether they are old pictures or new. If it had been a normal situation there would have been stacks of pictures and plenty of stories about their lives.

"There weren't any pictures of your parents because it was too dangerous to display them. The people who raised you had been selected to take care of you and protect you, and to keep their mouths shut. They had been your parents' trusted servants and would do anything to keep you from harm." His voice hiked.

"I don't believe you for a minute, damn you! If you think you can force me into marrying you, you're crazy!" she said, hands on her hips in a defiant stance. "Is the KGB after me for something? Am I going to see terrorists around every corner?"

"That would be so much easier," Mark said.

He appeared sad for a moment.

A soft knock on the outer door interrupted the hostile words flying between them.

Spencer entered the room as if their shouting match hadn't taken place. "Lunch is ready." His arm swept wide to the sitting room.

Alma was embarrassed at being caught in an argument. She wondered how much Spencer had heard, and what thoughts raced through his head from the other side of the door.

Did he already know about this betrothal? He most likely knew more about it than she did since he was Mark's trusted servant.

Turning pink, she glanced away from the man, feeling he read her every thought.

Well-mannered from an upper-class upbringing, Mark offered his arm to Alma.

She refused his arm and rushed out of the room, head held high.

Anger coursed through her; she couldn't believe the absurd things he had told her. Still fuming, she noticed he had left the connecting doors open as if planning to return to the other room.

Well, I'm not returning to that room.

That damn bedroom stirred emotions in her that were hard to control. She needed to get through this stupid lunch and back to the safety of work! Thinking of the predicament she had gotten herself into, Alma felt uneasy.

No one had seen Mark before and they didn't know their lunch plans. This house was far enough from the road or neighbors to prevent her from escaping—if it came to that.

With all these wild stories he told her, she wondered about his mental stability. Similar opinions competed for space in her mind, making her nervous and angry.

The table, set with fine china, held scrumptious looking food, but her appetite had vanished during the heated argument.

"Come now, let's not disappoint Cook. She prepared this meal especially for you." Mark scolded her like a pouting two-year-old.

"I'm not very hungry," she said acidly.

I have every right to all the feelings I'm experiencing at this minute.

Unbeknownst to her, he slipped a soothing suggestion inside her mind. Minutes later she picked up her spoon and dipped it into the delicate broth in the soup bowl. After the first sip, her appetite returned, allowing her to finish the broth and eat the light, fluffy quiche.

"Cook will be delighted that you did her meal justice." Mark stood. "Come. I want to show you something."

She allowed him to pull out her chair. Alma followed him back into the bedroom, to the table that held the picture of his parents.

Mark picked up another framed picture and handed it to Alma.

Her hands gripped the delicate, gilded frame and her eyes widened in disbelief.

The picture depicted a lovely red-haired woman with delicate white skin and green eyes. She stood beside a man with coal black hair and laughing brown eyes. He held a tiny red-haired baby in his arms.

Alma blinked as she recognized her parents. She didn't know how and she didn't question the fact.

Memories filtered through her mind, pictures racing behind her eyes as she gazed at the photo.

From the back of her mind, she recalled her mother's delicate voice saying something, but she couldn't quite grasp the memory to understand the words.

Tears crowded her eyes and spilled over onto the glass that protected the photograph.

Mark removed the picture from her hands and placed it on the table. He gathered Alma into his arms and held her close. Her arms wrapped around him as if she held him every day and she cried silent tears.

"Don't cry. There are so many things you don't remember, but you will in time. I will teach you everything." Mark nuzzled her neck, below her ear.

Passion stirred inside her as she lifted her lips to join his in a fiery kiss that left her gasping. He pulled his lips away and trailed kisses along her chin and down her neck to the opening of her dress.

A deep-throated moan escaped her lips; she clutched his arms and leaned backwards, her face a picture of rapture.

He was swift to gather her up in his arms, never taking his lips from her delicate flesh. He crossed the floor to the bed where he eased her down on the familiar cover. As he continued his passionate assault, her hands clung to his shoulders. His brushed his lips from side to side over her full lips, teasing her with his moist tongue.

He covered her with his body and moved one hand to the buttons on her dress and gained entry to the delights hidden below.

As his hand caressed her skin, Mark became impatient with the remaining obstacles. Turning over on his side to face her, his eyes stared into hers. "Let me make love to you, Alma," he rasped, his eyes glazed with passion.

Lost with the rapture, the need for his physical touch overruled all her other emotions. "Mark. Yes. Love me."

With deft fingers, he removed her remaining barrier of clothing and freed his own body of the encumbering articles. He tossed his clothes aside, not caring where they landed or what they might look like later.

Their bodies and minds melded as one. The experience was more than a sexual interlude; it was an awakening for Alma.

The living dream.

As Mark loved her physically, he also loved her mentally. He knew what results the passion would bring.

In a split second, their minds merged. He restored forgotten knowledge to Alma but controlled its release. He blocked the surge of memories, letting only a few filter through at a time. There would be time for more later.

Celibate for so long, Alma hungered for him. She wanted all the passion she experienced in the dreams. She needed total fulfillment. The ecstasy was almost unbearable.

A memory slipped into her mind; twice before she had experienced this wild, reckless passion: the conception of each of her sons.

She gasped with that knowledge.

The recollection lingered a minute longer, then vanished, leaving her to the burning passion and the climactic end. Face to face on the rumpled sheets, their minds mingled.

Mark savored the passion as his hand stroked the soft flesh along the curve of her waist and hip. Alma's hands toyed with the blond hair on his chest.

"Why did you wait so long to make love to me?" she whispered into his mind. "I now understand you could have arranged this anytime to suit you."

"Do you regret it?" Mark continued to caress her with his mind as he sidestepped the question.

"No, I don't. Stop it, Mark!"

Physically, he was innocent of any wrongdoing. Mentally, he was making love to her, avoiding her probing questions. He ignored her plea and turned her on her back, lowered his lips to hers, and brushed his hands over her responsive flesh.

Alma moaned with desire. She closed her eyes and gripped his shoulders, pulling him closer, wanting him again.

Physical and mental passion consumed her as his lips loved her.

Without warning a terrible face and strange words flashed through her mind. She yelped with fright as her heart pounded; she sensed an unknown danger. The face, hidden behind a gray hood, was frightening—old, weathered skin; a short, pointed beard, more gray than white. Dark piercing eyes in deep sockets; and a wide jagged scar along his right cheekbone.

"What is it?" Mark sensed her fear.

She panted with fear, her mind frozen, her teeth clenched—she couldn't answer.

Mark slipped inside her mind and caught the remnants of the vision.

"Asedi! Alma, look at me. Look at me!" he commanded urgently, gripping her chin in his hand. "There is too much for you to learn and no time to explain. I will fill in all the gaps, answer all your questions. Our minds will merge in a way you have never experienced before."

Wild, glazed eyes stared back at him, he didn't know if she heard him; he feared she was going into shock.

"Alma! Break away from him!" Mark shouted.

Finally, she blinked.

"Lie still, hold your eyes steady with mine and open the pathway between your mind and mine," he commanded.

Frightened, she followed his directions. She didn't know how she understood what to do, but it was clear.

He hovered over her body. His arms supported the weight from her delicate frame and her hands touched his chest.

Their eyes locked together; a stillness consumed the room.

Eons of history, knowledge, and information passed from his mind to hers. Alma's face went slack. Her hands dropped to her sides. Information slapped into place with a clacking sound in her head like a high-speed camera

Alma remembered things erased from her mind for her own protection when she was a child.

When the download of information was complete, he lowered his lips to hers and brushed lightly, from side to side.

As he kissed her, Alma stared up into Mark's eyes, understanding many things; others would take time to digest. He rolled off her body and swung his legs off the bed and sat.

Alma got to her knees. She held her head as her eyes zoned out. Dizziness overtook her.

Mark sat on the bed and drew her into his arms.

"It may be unsettling for a short time, but all the information will seat itself," he said.

Mark tilted her head back, gazed into her eyes and lowered his mouth to hers.

She shivered in response to the sensations that rushed through her body. He would always be able to command her body; they belonged together. He had the power to make her body sing, and no one else could ever accomplish that.

"So many years wasted," Alma said. Anger surfaced. "Why wasn't I told? Why keep me in the dark? Did you think you could hide me from Asedi forever?" she asked Mark.

He felt the roiling rage below her surface—all the deceit *for her own good.*

"I assumed there would be more time. I didn't think he would find you so soon, damn it," Mark answered.

"What about my sons? They're in danger, aren't they?" she asked. It will take time for her to sort all the information she had just absorbed. Things were leaping at her out of context, and until the knowledge was organized it would be difficult to understand the bits and pieces that were surfacing.

"OUR sons. They're my children. You understand that now, don't you?" he asked.

"Poor Jeff! I used him and I didn't even realize it. Did you kill him?" she asked, horrified.

"I'm no murderer. Believe it or not, his death was very premature; nature took its own course. You were supposed to get divorced before the second child was born," he said.

"We have a lot to accomplish in a short period of time. I hate to end this lovely session, but we have to change your life publicly so people don't become suspicious. I am already established here as a wealthy businessman. You, my dear, will marry me as fast as these barbaric laws will allow."

"People are going to think that's awfully strange," she said. "I don't date, and suddenly I'm going to get married? Be reasonable, Mark."

"Two weeks, tops. It has to be a whirlwind romance— Miss Icicle will have to melt!" he said. "I guess we'd better get going. I should get you back to your office. You've been gone long enough to start gossip, which works to our advantage."

"You like that, don't you?" She was still unsure of the situation.

"Yes. I'm a patient man, but there are things that are extremely taxing. Asedi's blunder worked to my advantage, but I wanted you to get to know me in the normal sense."

"You've got to be kidding, Mark. Earthlings do not make love with their minds—they fantasize, but in their heads, and those thoughts are never transferred physically.

"They don't have unusual powers at all. It's true, some are brilliant. Some even have limited capabilities of mind control of various types, but you were a breed apart. I knew you were different, and dangerous from the first minute you appeared in my dreams.

"There was nothing normal in the way you introduced yourself in that dream world," she scolded him.

"I had to see how you responded. Reena and Jetron were explicit regarding your memory loss. They wanted you safe and the only way to accomplish that, you had to appear like a normal Earth child. They never realized that the revolution on Kredo would erupt into a full-scale war, or it would last so long."

"But now your people need you. Your father is tired; he can no longer rule as the strong leader he used to be. It will be dangerous.

"Even though Asedi lost the uprising and was banished with his small band of followers, he left others behind we can't identify. All of them are your enemies. It was only a matter of time before he found you. There are only so many choices in the galaxy," Mark said.

"My mother. She's dead, isn't she?" Tears rimmed Alma's emerald eyes. The knowledge had surfaced. A single year of memories from her infancy had to last a lifetime.

"I'm sorry, Alma. She longed for you but wouldn't take the chance of bringing you back to Kredo until she knew it was safe. How she agonized for you! She felt cheated that she never had the opportunity to hold her grandsons," he said with a fierce voice.

"Damn that evil lunatic, Asedi! We lived in such harmony before the revolution. He wanted power. Keeper of the Keys wasn't enough for him; he wanted to rule the planet."

"Keeper of the Keys? That's where his support came from, isn't it? He freed any criminal that would follow him into battle!" She nodded in understanding.

"Ecko, the prison moon. What a perfect secret. Because he was the Keeper, he was the only one who made regular trips there. Who warned father?"

"A man your father had sentenced for a terrible crime. The man brutally killed a rival, consumed with jealousy for a woman who wasn't even his.

"Your father gave him a long term, but the man didn't resent it. He understood his sentence and remained loyal to your father. After hearing of Asedi's plan, he enlisted in the evil group to learn as much as he could.

"When the time was right, he notified your father. The poor man was discovered and killed by Asedi's fanatics, but not until after the revolution was well underway.

"At least we had been pre-warned. Otherwise there's no telling what the outcome might have been. The fighting is over, but the worst is still to come.

"Your father needs you now. He still mourns your mother's death and blames himself for it. He wasn't responsible; there was no way to prevent what happened. She refused to leave his side and was killed by a knife meant for him.

"Your mother's death ended the long strife on our planet. Everyone loved her and her death stunned the world. Asedi's followers no longer saw the glory in following him. All but a few deserted him without a strong arm of support. Your father only banished him; he should have sentenced the maniac to death!" Mark said.

"Where exactly is Kredo?" Alma asked.

"In the Karona solar system," Mark said.

Chapter 5

Wednesday. This man had only been in her life for a day and a half in the flesh, plus the two-and-a-half weeks of dreams. It seemed like a lifetime and everything in her life turned upside down by his appearance.

The Miss Icicle days were behind her, along with struggling to survive. A much more urgent conflict had begun.

Alma arrived back at her office at three forty-five with Mark in tow. "Hold my calls," she told Molly.

Molly almost choked, all agog over her boss's companion. She barely sputtered out an answer. He was a ten plus on the man-watchers scale in her book. Molly seemed mystified over the abrupt change in her boss—and the almost four-hour lunch!

Molly sat on the edge of her chair as she watched the attractive couple stop at Alma's office.

Determined to change Alma's reputation immediately, Mark drew her into an intimate embrace and thoroughly kissed her for the benefit of gossip. He thought the news would run like wildfire once he left and Alma was inside her office with the door closed.

"No matter how much work you have, leave on time to-day and don't bring anything home with you." Mark ran his fingers along her jawline.

"Let the information I gave you surface. That will only happen if you aren't bogged down with business matters running around in your head. Concentrate on Kredo and let this other stuff go."

Nodding, Alma kissed him lightly on the lips.

As Mark approached Molly's desk, he turned towards Alma and blew her a kiss. He winked at Molly as he left.

Molly went through several shocked seconds of stunned silence. She grabbed the phone and called her best friend in purchasing as soon as the elevator doors closed behind Mark and Alma was in her office.

"Beverly! You will not believe this because I can hardly get my head around it and I witnessed it. My boss has caught the man of the year!" Molly confided.

"This guy is gorgeous! Go look out the window and catch a look at him. Blue suit, blond hair. A hunk from the front and back!"

Gossip spreads faster than any germ in large corporations, and Hunter and Bloomfield had no immunity to the dreadful disease.

Molly started the chain reaction and called two more of her work friends. By morning, even the guard would have inside information about the romance.

Alma left work at five. She thought about everything she needed to do. She needed time to focus, to prepare for her new life. As she walked to the elevator, she noticed stares from two people. Mark predicted correctly, her reputation skyrocketed!

The elevator ride was an experience. Everyone smiled at her like a bunch of idiots. If they kept it up, they'd all need surgery to remove the ludicrous grins. She couldn't wait to get to the sanctuary of her car.

I must have been a cold fish without realizing it. I can't get over the way these people are acting. All this because of one man? Brother! Would this have warranted the same treatment if I hadn't been so reserved? There's so much to sort through.

The boys whooped it up when their mother's car approached the circular drive early the second day in a row. The attendant walked them out to the car, greeted Alma and said goodbye to Cody and Jamie after they settled into the car seats. Turning in her seat to face them, Alma blew a kiss to each of her sons.

"Hi, kids. Did you guys have a nice day today?" she asked.

"George Montgomery didn't come to school today, Mom. He got bit on the leg by a dog. I'll bet it has rabies," Cody said, excited. "Do you think George will get rabies, Mom?"

"That's awful! Was it George's dog or a stray, Cody?" Alma asked.

"It was Miss Mackenzie's dog. You remember her, don't you, Mom? She's that old lady who lives next door to George and always complains about everything," Cody said.

"Now, Cody. Miss Mackenzie has a right to complain. Georgie terrorizes that poor woman. You should realize that Miss Mackenzie isn't married and has never had children of her own. She doesn't understand that little boys are very curious, and her poodle isn't used to children either." Alma defended the elderly woman and her poodle. "Get the facts, Cody. Don't take your friend's word for everything. There are two sides to every story."

Cody fumed. His news flash had been crushed by his mother's common sense.

"You're awfully quiet, Jamie. Did you have a good day?" Alma asked her younger son. She hoped he wasn't coming down with something. The only time he was quiet was when he didn't feel good.

"I had an awful dream at nap time today, Mom," the youngster said.

"Yeah, Mom. Jamie yelled in his sleep at naptime." Cody's face lit with excitement.

"Poor baby! What did you dream about, can you remember?" Alma asked.

"An evil old man is after us, Mom!" Jamie said matter-of-factly.

Tires screeched as Alma slammed her foot on the brakes. Remembering the perils of traffic, she put her directional lights on. She looked in the rear-view mirror and eased over to the shoulder on the right side of the road before she caused an accident.

Alma slammed the car into park and turned to the back seat and stared at her younger child.

"Tell me what happened, Jamie. Try to remember everything." She was talking too fast to sound natural. Alma heard her voice high and tight as she tried to maintain a steely calm.

"An awful old man wearing an old gray bathrobe looked in my head, Mom! He never said anything. He just looked around in my head for something." The young boy cried. "I don't know what he wanted."

"Oh, Jamie!" Alma didn't say anymore. She turned around in her seat and thought for a few minutes. "Let's get home, kids."

She waited for a kind driver to let her back into the flow of traffic. "On second thought, we should go over to my friend's house. He lives close by and would love to meet you two."

Inside her head, she ranted wildly, furiously and scared for her children.

Alma veered the car off the main street and turned down the two-lane road. After several minutes of scrutinizing the side area, she found the hidden, private entrance and turned into the tree-lined drive.

"Wow! Look at that!" Cody exclaimed as the house came into view up ahead.

"Is your friend rich, Mom?" Jamie asked, forgetting his fright.

"I know who lives here, Mom," Cody said, excited.

Alma looked in the rear-view mirror at her older son; she asked skeptically, "Who lives here, Cody?"

"This is Mark's house!" the boy said, excited.

Alma's imagination ramped into high gear. She couldn't escape this web. Her children probably had more information about this secret life than she did. The frightening kaleidoscope would soon flip another scenario through its lens.

"Cody, when did you meet Mark?" A slight quiver slipped into the last word.

"I'm not sure how to explain it, Mom. I've always known him, but he's never here. What I mean is he's here, but not in person," the boy tried to explain.

"Do you mean in a dream, perhaps?" Alma asked, helping the boy.

"Yes, that's it!" he said. "Mark's my real father."

Alma clenched the wheel, stunned.

When had this all begun? How had the boys known all along before I did and why hadn't they ever said or asked anything?

She shook her head, not quite sure whether she was confused or angry; she wasn't going to question them anymore. There didn't seem to be any point.

She thought of the perils that lurked ahead and was glad Cody knew Mark. It would make the transition easier, but she didn't like the idea of Jamie being involved. Why this child? He was much too young! Alma gritted her teeth in anger, cursed silently and pulled the car up in front of the steps.

The front door opened. Spencer walked down the stone steps and greeted Alma. "What a splendid surprise, Miss Alma! And I see you've brought the two tots along," Spencer said. "Come along now, boys and we'll find out what Cook has just taken out of the oven."

Taken aback, Alma stared dumbfounded at Spencer as he took the boys, one in each hand, and walked up the steps. She regained her senses and hurried after them.

How did Spencer fit in the picture?

He always took things in stride and seemed to understand how everything fit into place.

"Master Mark is in the drawing room; I expect he's waiting for you," Spencer said as he headed in the opposite direction, engrossed in a conversation with her two sons.

Does he expect me to remember where the room is after only one visit?

Second door on the right, he said in her mind.

Startled, she stared after him, trying to fit another piece of the puzzle together. In a huff, Alma entered without knocking on the closed door and had to restrain herself from slamming it shut.

He knows I'm here. Why waste time on formalities?

A picture of satisfaction, Mark lounged on the sofa, left ankle on his right knee. One arm was slung along the back of the blue, bold print velvet Chippendale sofa, his jacket removed, tie loosened.

Their eyes met and locked. He felt the sparks of anger emanating from her and figured out the problem by peeking into her head.

"It's only been a little over two hours. You can't expect everything to fall into place, Alma," Mark said, softly. "It will take time."

"Asedi has been probing Jamie's mind. He's scared! What next? And while we're playing twenty questions, why didn't you tell me my children were already acquainted with you?" Alma's voice rose.

"OUR children! A father has certain rights to his sons, Alma!" Mark's teeth clenched in a tight jaw.

"Damn it, don't you understand, Mark? They're children! They don't understand what's going on. What did you tell them about Jeff, who I assumed they understood was their father? Don't you think it would have been a good idea to let me in on this little secret? I almost wrecked the car on the way home when Cody told me who you were."

"I told them what they could understand. When they grow up, they will get the whole story. I've taught them how to protect themselves in case of an emergency," he said.

Alma was so angry she sputtered. The words wouldn't make sense so she stayed quiet.

"Try to understand. They may not figure things out right away, but in a crisis, they will keep their cool and use the measures I have taught them. It's all stored in their memories. Their safety is my number one concern. Your mind will digest the information over time. You need to rest to absorb what is necessary for the present."

Drained from the argument, her shoulders slumped.

Mark rose from the sofa and crossed the space that separated them. He drew her to him and pressed his lips to her soft, shiny hair and comforted her with his nearness.

A feeling of security enveloped Alma. She put her fears and anger behind her, she slipped her arms under his and held him tightly.

Was it possible to experience peace and dread at the same time?

She wondered. If so, she was experiencing both.

"You're not in my mind. Why?" She was confused with the sudden reversal of tactics.

"Because you're here and you're mine. I don't have to send you dream sequences to control your emotions, which I did not like doing. That was necessary to communicate with you, and at the time you were scared and didn't want to listen. I did not use any type of control over you when we made love in the dreams. That was your own free will," he said.

"Let's go find out what the kids are getting into before we get into big trouble."

"Does that mean you won't be sneaking inside my mind anymore?" she asked.

"I didn't say that." A devilish smile formed on his face.

They left the room arm in arm and walked toward the kitchen where Spencer had taken the boys. All talking stopped; all eyes flew to Mark and Alma.

The stout woman in the white apron wiped her hands on her apron and smiled; Preston and Spencer withdrew from the table, knowing a crucial time was near.

The boys stared in silence at their mother and Mark. Alma thought they were assessing the situation. They were seeing Mark in the flesh for the first time and digesting their emotions.

At that minute, Alma realized her sons might not be the typical little kids she had understood them to be only hours ago. She didn't understand how they differed, but she assumed she would find out soon enough and the thought frightened her.

Will they still be interested in playing with cars and trucks, or were Kredon children simply small advanced adults?

Would they treat each other differently?

Questions flew through her mind, increasing her uncertainty.

"Cody, Jamie, come say hello to Mark, your father. You've seen him before, many times; you've just never met him in person," she explained.

"Mark and I are getting married soon so there is a lot to do. I'm sure you understand because your father has been talking to you in secret. He can explain things much easier, and he didn't want me to get upset."

"I told you dreams come true!" Cody boasted, turning to his younger brother. Neither had budged.

"Cody, this isn't the same as dreaming about your favorite TV character being your father. The dreams where you saw me were forced dreams. I put them in your mind because I have that ability. You didn't just dream me up and poof, I appeared today," Mark explained. "Circumstances wouldn't allow me to appear any other way, or any sooner. We'll talk more later, okay?"

Both boys nodded.

Turning to Alma, he said, "Will you stay tonight?"

"We didn't come prepared," she said, uncertain.

"Everything you need is here. Let me show you the rooms," Mark said as he led her out of the kitchen.

They walked down the hall to the massive stairs and climbed up to the second floor.

The first room they entered held a rustic colonial bed covered with a dark green and gold comforter and accenting pillows. The window seat was covered with the same material; a fireplace graced one wall with its teak mantle. Brass accents and antiques filled the room.

They crossed the room to an open doorway. A combination large closet-playroom connected to a large bathroom, which in turn connected to another closet-playroom and adjoining bedroom.

This room was furnished similar to the one Alma had just left, but with dark blue and silver bedding and accessories.

The closets were filled with clothes, the shelves filled with the same toys the boys played with all the time.

She recognized a few worn items that were the boys' everyday favorites and she was relieved that Mark had such insight.

"You've planned this out thoroughly, haven't you?" Alma asked in wonderment.

"I know my sons," Mark said.

"Yes, I bet you do. Mark, will I ever feel not human?" she asked.

Where was all this knowledge?

"Alma, try to understand. You are human. Kredons are merely sophisticated, powerfully intelligent people who have learned to use their minds beyond Earthling intelligence. Our race has been around longer than the Earth itself. It will all come to you, I promise."

He choked on a laugh. "Come on, I want to show you your sitting room. I'm sure you'll like it."

They left the boys' rooms to continue down the hall toward Mark's rooms. They entered a door before his. Alma was delighted with the lovely sitting room furnished in Louis XVI style.

The pretty writing desk and chair, the medallion-back love seat with its peach and white striped upholstery, a matching chair, and the wonderful Persian rug.

Alma crossed the room to a door, with Mark following. She hesitated then opened the door to discover a large dressing room-closet filled to capacity with an assortment of women's clothing and accessories.

She had never owned this many clothes in her entire life. And that was counting all the things that had been given away over the years due to style changes or size differences.

What a rainbow of color!

She scanned the dresses, skirts, slacks, jackets and shirts. There were scarves, belts, purses and shoes to match everything.

Three jewelry boxes contained everything she could ever want from colorful costume jewelry to beautiful crafted gold and silver chains, pins, earrings—everything for today's modern woman.

Drawn to a door opposite her, as a moth to its wedding with the flame, she crossed the room and opened the door.

Mark's bedroom.

Our bedroom.

Of course.

A feeling of comfort swept over her. Any anger melted away. She understood more and more.

The boys are safe here. I'm safe. Today was the last day of the daycare center.

As the situations ran through her mind, she assumed her house had already been emptied of personal possessions.

Those things would be brought to this house and stored, then the house would be sold.

Truly a different person now, she knew her life would never be the way it had been before. There was so much to do. She had enormous responsibilities now.

Many people depended upon her; her father needed her. She would have to go to Kredo soon. The cycle here was nearing an end, and she understood why she couldn't wait two weeks to pacify the people she worked with. She was already planning the change.

Tomorrow she would talk to her boss; the company would survive without her. She must make an appearance at the house and still the neighbors' suspicions.

Since she was a private person and didn't socialize with them that much, everything would flow smoothly. It was time for her new life to take over completely, time to tie up all loose ends.

Mark stood silently at her side and observed her reactions, knowing the outcome of that step through the doorway to his room.

Their room, now.

Knowledge raced through her mind, but only a tiny fraction of what would filter down over time. Meditative rest was important now; he would teach her that later tonight.

He wanted her right then but held himself in check, waiting for the evening to come to an end. Tonight was not the night he would have chosen to begin parenting in the flesh, but he knew his sons would behave.

Chapter 6

Dinner had been an awkward, quiet affair for the four imposters, as they were unsure of what to say out loud. The house and furnishings were of Earth, but the inhabitants hailing from Kredo, a planet in a distant galaxy recovering from a revolution.

Alma wondered how someone might suspect they were not from Earth if there had never been any clues. She let her mind wander back to her childhood. She never doubted who she was or suspected anything unusual regarding her upbringing. She never had a reason to consider that she was unusual.

School hadn't been any different for her. She had whizzed through with straight A's; a lot of kids did.

Once in junior high, then again in high school she tried flunking so she didn't look so smart to the other kids. But she never got the hang of writing incorrect answers.

If she copied work from a classmate, she always corrected the mistakes, thereby helping the person and still getting her A.

Being stupid was not in her genes or her life path so she gave up trying to change. After talking it over with the school counselor, she discovered that it was okay to make A's.

School was easy for a lot of people and she was one of them, the counselor had explained. After she understood that and the reasons the popular kids made fun of her, she was okay.

Alma daydreamed through dinner and reflected on the lie that her marriage had been. She recalled the times that Mark had taken Jeff's place and had made love to her.

She remembered those passionate times, now intertwined with the fresh memory of his recent lovemaking. She mentally flogged herself for being so dense. She should have figured out that something was not right.

How can anyone live without that type of passion? Why would anyone want to slog through the everyday routine of life and never experience true love?

She didn't understand how she had tolerated her marriage before those precious encounters, and she realized she couldn't possibly settle for anything less now.

You should never marry for a lifetime of friendship. She found out the lack of love in a relationship could eventually turn to misery or hate. That special element had to be there for the marriage to last.

"When do we go back home?" Alma asked.

Both boys perked up at once.

"Soon. You need to be prepared to step into your father's shoes. Although you and I will be married and our children will seal the bond, you—and only you—can rule the people. This is decreed by our laws and customs—the firstborn inherits and rules." Mark looked first to Alma, then nodded to Cody.

"I will be at your side to guide you. I have the training from being in your father's court over the years and we both have the breeding of our families—that royal blood." Mark paused momentarily and leaned forward.

"Stop fearing your role. You are a natural for the position, a mentor for Cody. I will not let anything harm you."

"Oh, Mark, it's just so overwhelming. I have all these Earthly fears and feelings crammed into my skull, and I'm scared. I want to be a regular person again."

"Let's go into the library. I need to show you something." Mark pushed his chair back and stood.

Everyone left the room and walked the short distance to the library. They were amazed at the number of books on the floor to ceiling shelves.

Mark steered them over to a paneled wall and drew their attention to three knots in the wood.

He fit his fingers into the slight indents and pressed, which caused the wood to separate. A large room was revealed with many pieces of strange equipment.

Mark pointed out each item. He explained that the transmitting and receiving devices were so superior that messages would never be detected by any of the scientific equipment or radar of any government on Earth.

"Earth is still centuries behind in development," he explained. "Although we send mental messages, we occasionally need to send other communications.

"The alagon ray isn't detected, other than as extremely fast, white light. If the military intercepted one of the message rays they'd never be able to decode it. They wouldn't even guess it was something to decode, they are so far behind in technological advances.

"Earth has another two hundred years to go before they even notice the rays. By that time, they will be space pioneers with more knowledge of the surrounding universe. Maybe they will stop making those ridiculous alien movies."

Mark rolled his eyes upward, making the boys giggle.

For Alma's peace of mind, he asked, "Do you remember what I taught you two to protect yourselves?"

"We're supposed to think a bubble, right, dad?" Jamie asked.

"That's right, Jamie. Project a bubble around you. Make it so hard that no one can get inside to you. It's important to remember that part. Someone can transport you in your protective bubble, but they can't get inside it, or remove it.

"There are people who may try to hurt you, and you need to protect yourselves until we can get to you. Only your mother or I, or Preston and Spencer will ever come for you.

"Never take your bubble shield down no matter what anyone tells you. Bad people are sneaky and will try to trick you. They will even lie to you and tell you all sorts of stories, or they may even tell you that your mother and I are dead. Never believe any story a stranger tells you. You'll discover the truth.

"Another thing I want to explain is that these people may have someone put on a mask so they look like your mother or me. You can do a mind probe and look deep inside their brain to see who they are, or you can surround them with a mind bubble they can't see. That will allow you to see their real identity.

"You are capable of doing many things—the things I taught you while you slept," Mark said. "Above all else, protect each other and be cautious of who you befriend.

"Trust your intuition. If your brain gives you a little tingle down your spine, its telling you to be suspicious and not trust that person. Check them out first, for your own peace of mind and safety."

They left the secret room and the boys skipped off to get ready for bed. They acted as if they had been raised in the house.

Finished with his demonstration, Mark secured the panels and walked arm in arm with Alma out the double doors toward the polished stairway.

"Will they remember everything in a crisis?" Alma asked. "They are awfully young."

"They're young, but they have brilliant minds. Yes, they will remember in a crisis," Mark nodded.

"I will instruct you on how the equipment works. It will be important for you to understand how to send a message back home in case of an emergency. Did you notice the aluminum ring on the desk?" he asked.

"Yes. I don't have a clue what any of those things were. The ring looked like an embroidery hoop," she said.

"That was a holographic message holder. All you need to do is project your message and run your fingers around the inside of the rim once, and your message is preserved," he explained.

Her face lit with a wicked thought.

"No X-rated messages. Anyone who has access to the room can get the message. Just consider it as if it was a modern version of the old pink telephone message pads, but much more refined."

"I'll say! Look at all the writing efforts saved. Never mind that, think of the trees that are saved! Oh, this planet is so far behind Kredo," she exclaimed.

"Earth is young; she'll grow up in time," he said.

They walked up the gleaming stairs together. Alma reflected on how comfortable she was in Mark's home. Their home. She belonged there; she and the boys felt settled. It was a good feeling.

They climbed to the landing and headed toward the boys' rooms.

Jamie and Cody were getting ready for bed and didn't appear to mind that this was not their usual place to sleep.

I wondered how they'd react about leaving our house. They seemed to have accepted their new lives without question, probably because of the shared, secret relationship with their father.

Alma hoped her adjustment would be as easy. She mulled over private concerns.

The risks were great.

Her father. What was he like? She pulled his image into her mind and pictured a formidable ruler, but that didn't fit the man in the gilded frame.

My father looks kind, gentle and proud. Will my memories come flooding back all at once?

She thought they might. How she hated the knowledge of her mother being dead! She had been robbed of that love and she wanted to get even with those responsible for taking her mother away from her. She had tons to sort out in her head.

Alma and Mark went through the ritual together of tucking each boy into bed for the first time.

"Good night, Mom. I love you," Jamie said.

"Night Jamie, pleasant dreams," Alma hugged and kissed him.

"Good night, dad. I love you, too," Jamie said to Mark.

"I love you, too, son. Go to sleep now. We'll see you in the morning." Mark was touched. He was a real father now, not just a dream tripper.

Mark shut off the light. He and Alma left Jamie and walked through the doors that connected to Cody's room.

Cody yawned as he was climbing into bed.

Alma pulled the covers up around his shoulders and kissed his cheek as Cody bid them goodnight.

"Good night, Mom. Don't worry, everything will work out; our father's here now. Night, Dad, I love you," Cody said.

"Good night son." Mark ruffled Cody's hair.

They left the room and walked the short distance to their suite. Alma kicked her shoes off in her dressing room, then continued to her sitting room and curled up on the pretty sofa.

Minutes later, Mark joined her, carrying two glasses of wine. He handed one to Alma.

She sipped the delicate nectar while peering at him through lowered lashes.

He sank onto the sofa beside her.

Silence engulfed the room as they sat enjoying the wine and solitude.

Mark slipped into her mind and kissed her lips passionately. He then trailed kisses down her neck, flicking his tongue across her collar bone, attacking her senses to where she almost dropped her wine glass.

He removed the delicate crystal from her shaking fingers and placed both glasses on a table beside the sofa then turned toward her.

He followed his mental sensual attack with physical delights.

Alma came close to swooning in his arms, so heady was his passion.

He emitted an overpowering sensuality that was captivating. His lovemaking couldn't be compared to any other form of ecstasy.

As his hands glided across her body, followed by his hungry mouth, tiny passionate sounds escaped her lips.

He unbuttoned the colorful dress, then released the front hook that held her wispy bra together.

Her nipples strained toward his lowering head, waiting for the ultimate contact of lips and flesh. Her hands pulled his head toward its goal with an impatience that couldn't be stifled.

Unable to tolerate the teasing any longer, she dragged Mark's head away from her throbbing breasts to kiss his warmed lips.

In an instant, he pulled his mouth free, rose to his feet and scooped her up in his arms. Mark walked through the connecting dressing room to the huge bedroom and kicked the door closed. He then crossed the floor and deposited Alma on her feet beside the bed. He grasped the opened front of her dress and slipped the material off her shoulders.

Mark covered her smooth white skin with kisses and followed the material down her arms, easing the dress past her hips and letting it fall to the floor.

The dainty bra followed. He knelt in front of her and kissed her mound through the lacy panties. He slipped his fingers through the waistband and slid them past her thighs. She stepped out of them.

With his hands on her hips, he brushed his lips across her body. A moan escaped her lips as she gripped his shoulders tightly. First for support from the heady feeling, then she pulled him upward, demanding him to stand before her, which he did.

She clumsily unbuttoned the first two buttons on his shirt when he pushed her hands aside and yanked open his shirt, sending the buttons flying. Next, he removed the blue suit pants, then the remaining pieces of clothing.

They melted into each other's arms. Lips meeting lips. Curves molding together. Getting closer was crucial.

Mark lifted Alma onto the king-sized bed and covered her body with his. His lovemaking started with slow, tantalizing kisses beginning with her passion-swollen lips.

As he made love to her, he brought an awareness into her life she never realized even existed. He taught her the meaning of fiery passion that evolved from true love. The mounting passion exploded like a dying planet in the galaxy which left them clinging to each other, gasping.

Without speaking, he rolled over and turned Alma on her side, tucking her body close to his. He kissed her creamy white shoulder and rested his lips against her skin and sighed deeply, breaking the contented silence.

"We were both cheated of so much. Your marrying that man was an accident that no one expected. When Elu and Dresdon—your Aunt and Uncle—died, your father decided to see what you would do on your own.

"You were very young, not quite eighteen, and we never realized how sheltered your life had been. He never figured a man would waltz into your life and change the plan. I was supposed to make an entrance then.

"I was furious at first. I sulked like a spoiled child and stayed away. Your father warned me of the danger of the possibility of you having children by that backward Earthling, so I came here and 'got involved.'

"I don't know how you lived such a meager existence, Alma. It was a nightmare for me. I saw EVERYTHING that went on in your life." He hesitated to let his words sink in.

"Everything?" she asked in horror, turning to face him. Memories flew through her mind in a rush.

I was a virgin and sex hadn't been on my mind until my wedding night.

She blushed as the scene replayed in her mind.

Is there no privacy in my life?

"Everything!" He gritted his teeth. "I couldn't stand it any longer with that bumbling idiot pawing you over. I took control of him that one night and showed you the meaning of passion before he ruined you.

"It was a mistake; your father was so furious he almost sent me into exile. What I did was inexcusable. Then when you became pregnant I performed a gene check one night when you were asleep. I had to know if the child was mine."

"What if Cody hadn't been your baby?"

"You would not have been allowed to have anything but a Kredon baby—my baby! And I was very much a father, Alma. I was with Cody every single night!"

Mark projected a vision to Alma that shocked her.

He walked the floor with Cody in his arms.

He changed a wet diaper.

He gave Cody a bottle.

"I wondered how it was possible to have this perfect child that let me sleep almost every night. You were there all that time? Why? Why did this have to happen like this?" she demanded, tears rimming her eyes.

"Why didn't you trust me with the knowledge? Asedi would have had to check every person on the planet to find me unless you led him right to me. I don't see any reason why I was left in the dark.

"All those years I should have had a mother and a father. I could have been training for my position so when the day came, I would have been ready to step into it."

"Don't cry, Alma. There was no other way at the time. I didn't think your marriage would last very long. After Cody was born, he never made love to you again. He was always polite, always treated you and the baby right, but it was as if he had no interest anymore. You know the rest.

"Your friends' party was my chance to make love to you again. That was the only other time until just recently. I guess he figured he made love to you when he was drunk because he never doubted Jamie's parentage for a minute."

"Mark, *that man* and *he* had a name—it was Jeff! He may have been inferior by Kredon standards, but he was a warm, caring person. We needed each other at a challenging time in our lives. We weren't blindly in love. We filled each other's time with friendship and common interests.

"Jeff and I never had a sexual thing for each other, and to be perfectly honest, I doubt if either one of us considered having sex in the marriage. It just happened." Alma calmed down with the silence.

"I'll never let anyone get in between us again. I will not share, Alma, and I will not tolerate! There isn't room for a third person. I will not share my sons with another man!"

Mark's blue eyes mirrored his stormy emotions, then softened and closed as he lowered his lips to hers.

Alma wrapped her arms around his neck and continued to close the gap between them. She crushed him to her, received his kisses, and returned them, encouraging his ardor until their passion boiled over and consumed them.

Their lovemaking was powerful; a pounding, intense consumption of love, with each of them making declarations in short, gasping statements.

Sleep captured them almost immediately afterwards, thrusting each into a satisfied, languid state of mind.

Sunlight drifted in through the wispy curtains, nagging Alma's eyes with a brightness she was no longer able to ignore.

Her first thought was of total comfort, both physical and mental. She gazed upon the man beside her and she recalled the earlier night of wild passion. As the memory rolled in her mind, her heart beat quicker.

I want that passion for the rest of my life.

"God, Mark. I'm so afraid."

Mark stirred out of his sleep-state, turned and kissed her shoulder. "It will always be there Alma. I'll always be there, beside you." He pulled her into the curve of his warm body.

"I've got to get up and get ready for work," she reminded him. "It's only Thursday. I'm giving my notice today."

"You're late. It's almost eight." He grinned. "I was supposed to teach you about meditation last night. I guess the lesson will have to wait until tonight, so don't tempt me."

Alma pulled away from his warmth and turned to face him. "Mark, if anything should ever happen to me, I want you to know I love you. I'm not the same Alma Weston anymore; I know I've changed. I don't quite understand it, but in some way I'm different. It's like an emotional impact."

Tears rimmed her green eyes. "There's so much to do, so much risk involved. Protect the boys at all costs."

Mark sat up, the sheet slipped, partially exposing his lower body. He pulled her against him and held her naked body to his; her cheek rested on his chest.

"Everything will be all right, darling. Nothing will destroy what we have. Come on now, let's get moving and stop this talk of gloom and doom. You've got to shower and dress for work. Coffee is on its way up here now." He slapped her on the butt.

As she bounced off the bed, Alma hit him with a pillow and headed for the bathroom. After her shower, she disappeared, clad in a towel, into the enormous closet-dressing room.

It was difficult to decide what to wear. There were so many wonderful choices—she could not fault Mark for his taste in women's clothing.

Alma chose a royal blue dress. The white shoes and purse were a perfect match. She sat at the well-lit vanity and applied light makeup.

After a final inspection, she joined Mark in his sitting room where coffee, juice and an English muffin awaited her. She savored the aroma of the coffee. Alma sat beside Mark on the rich brown leather sofa. Her coffee was perfect.

How did he know I took one sugar and a little milk?

She discarded the question and ate the muffin, finished the juice and indulged in the wonderful coffee.

"I'm going to have to leave now," she said regretfully.

"Preston is waiting by the car." He kissed her goodbye. "He already took the boys to school."

Chapter 7

The silent ten-minute drive through the winding, congested roads to the office was wisely spent. Alma planned how she would announce her upcoming marriage to her boss. She gazed out the window as Preston drove the car toward her workplace. Alma saw people gawking at the luxurious car, wondering who she was.

She turned her mind back to the problem.

The whole company will be shocked beyond belief so my story has to be a good one to convince the speculators.

Alma predicted that jerk Doug Harris would start a rumor she was pregnant and had to get married so the numbers totaled up right.

She seethed.

Who gives a damn about such things anymore? Those small minds of ten or twenty years ago are the minority. There's thousands of single mothers who choose to raise their babies alone.

Preston pulled the silver Rolls Royce up to the curb. Alma enjoyed the envious looks her coworkers gave her as he helped her out of the car.

Several coworkers arrived at the same time and gawked at the sight of Alma descending from the chauffeur-driven Rolls Royce. They whispered among themselves as they walked across the parking lot. She smiled at them and turned to Preston.

"I'll call you when I'm ready to leave this afternoon," she said.

"No need. Just mentally send your message to me," Preston said.

Alma blinked. "Oh!"

Preston winked. "Our secrets." He touched the brim of his hat, gave a slight bow, and returned to the car, maneuvering the sleek automobile toward home.

Alma entered the building and smiled at John, sitting at his usual desk, checking badges. His gray guard's uniform was spotless, as usual, his face ready with a warm, friendly smile.

"Morning, Ms. Weston! It's a dandy of a day." John greeted her with his usual enthusiasm.

"Make sure you get outside for some of this wonderful sunshine, John," Alma said.

She flashed her badge and walked to the elevator. When she pushed the button, the car responded at once. The doors slid open.

What? No cranky elevator this time?

Not being able to make a quiet escape, three chatty people followed her inside and resorted to whispers and facial expressions upon seeing her.

They zipped up to the fifth floor in nothing flat.

Have I gained magical control over these minor things in my life?

Alma was thankful for the speed—she was uncomfortable being stared at by her coworkers.

She greeted Molly and headed to her office. Without her laptop in her arms this morning, opening the door was a cinch. Alma dumped her purse in the desk drawer then turned to her calendar to check the day's schedule.

Good, no surprises on the calendar. Normal day. Except there's nothing normal about my life anymore.

She picked up her coffee cup. She stopped at Molly's desk. "Is Ron here yet?"

"He's in his office," Molly answered.

"Hold his calls. I need to talk to him."

"Sure thing, Ms. Weston."

Alma got coffee and headed to Ron's office. She tapped on his open door.

"Morning, Alma!" Ron appeared cheerful.

"Good Morning, Ron. Can you spare a minute?"

"I sure can." He put his papers aside.

Alma closed the door and slipped into one of the tan leather-looking chairs in front of his desk. "There's no easy way to break this to you, Ron, but I wanted to tell you first thing this morning instead of getting on your calendar."

The smile vanished from Ron's face and was replaced with knitted brows as he interrupted her. "What's the matter, Alma? Are you in some kind of trouble?"

"Oh no, it's nothing like that. I'm getting married next week and wanted you to be the first to know!"

There. It was out.

"WHAT!" Ron yelped in disbelief, his face distorted in shock.

Molly typed like lightning at her desk. She paused, scrunched her brow trying to read Ron's handwriting and picked up her yellow highlighter and marked a sentence.

Her head shot up as she heard Ron's exclamation through the closed door.

"Uh oh. Something's going on."

"I told you it would be a shock! Stay calm and let me explain. Drink your coffee before it gets cold," Alma coaxed.

"I'm sure at least twenty questions are ping-ponging through your head so let me give you the details. His name is Mark St. Claire, and I knew him long before my marriage to Jeff.

"We used to be an item, and he walked back into my life a few weeks ago and swept me off my feet. He's afraid if we wait, I'll run off and marry someone else again, so we're getting married next week."

She prayed he wouldn't discover the lie.

If he got out his calculator he'd see how young I would have had to be when Mark and I were 'an item.' He'd see through this charade.

"Good lord! You really know how to pull off a surprise, don't you?" he said, stunned. "Will you want time off?"

"Mark is a successful businessman so there's no need for me to work. I'll type up my notice, effective next Friday. I want to raise my boys, then pursue an education if that's what I want. I hate to leave you in a bind, but next Friday will be my last day." Her courage was ebbing.

"I never considered THIS situation. I'm stunned but thrilled for you. You've had a rough time, Alma, and I'm glad things worked out this way. When will I be meeting this man?"

"The next time Mark comes up here I'll introduce you. You'll see he's the right man for me."

"I didn't mean to sound like a concerned parent," he said.

"Sure, you did! Listen, Ron, without your support over the years I'm not sure I would have survived! I appreciate your concern. It means a lot to me," she said. "You helped me through the roughest time in my life when Jeff died."

Ron sighed. "I was happy to step in, Alma. You were so lost, especially with two small children and no other family members."

"Thanks, Ron. I owe you so much and I'm grateful that you took charge and helped with the funeral arrangements and the dozens of details I wasn't capable of handling. I feel like I'm deserting you by leaving so suddenly like this, but I want this chance at happiness." Alma's face expressed her thanks.

"Don't ever feel bad about that, Alma. This is just a job, and a poor substitute for happiness," he replied.

"I'm going back to my office and try to put things in order," she said.

"Can I let the cat out of the bag or do you want to keep it a secret until Monday?"

"I won't spoil your fun. Tell Molly. She'll burn the messaging app with the news!" Alma said.

"Well, how's everything else going?" Ron asked.

"Evelyn turned in her notice. She can't stand working for Taylor anymore. This situation requires immediate action, Ron. Several complaints have already been filed," she said.

"I can't understand why he acts this way. If his wife knew the way he treated the women at the office, she'd bash him with the cast-iron skillet," Ron said.

"Mrs. Taylor is the most vocal advocate for women's rights around. If she ever heard what a chauvinist Lance was, it'd be all over for him. Let me talk to him and see if he changes his tune."

As Alma walked back to her office Molly's phone dinged.

She'll be in hysterics any minute now.

Molly knocked on Alma's door.

So soon!

She was carrying a large, wrapped box. "A delivery service just brought this for you, Ms. Weston! Where do you want it?"

Alma cleared a place for it on the desk. Puzzled, she opened the gift.

Molly squealed.

Alma scrunched her eyebrows. "Why are you going bonkers over a tan purse?" Alma lifted the purse out of the box. "This is nice, but…"

"OMG! That's a Chloe! I've seen Kate Moss with one that looks just like this, and hers was twelve hundred dollars!"

"Are you serious?" Alma asked. "Mark needs to tone it down."

"Oh, Ms. Weston, it's divine!" Molly caressed the leather. "Look, here's the card."

Alma dug the card out from the bottom of the box, Alma read the neat written lines: "Until tonight. All my love, Mark." She placed the card on the desk for Molly to read.

After several minutes of chattering, Molly bounded out of the office. Alma was sure she was on her way to Ron's office, where she would get the whole story. After she recovered from the news, she would most likely get on messenger and text Beverly the two scoops.

The Hunter and Bloomfield gossip mill may go up in smoke today. I wondered if the walls can take the pressure from the vibrations of gossip.

It was crazy for Mark to purchase the purse, but I realize he has a style to maintain and I have to accept it.

She placed the purse back in the box and set it on one of the guest chairs in front of her desk for everyone to see.

She sat at her desk, closed her eyes and concentrated. A vision of Mark sitting at the desk in his home office appeared inside her mind's eye. She went to him, slipped onto his lap and wrapped her arms around his neck. She lowered her lips to his, and captured him in an intense kiss.

As suddenly as she had appeared before him, she felt herself jerked back. She was stunned that she had accomplished such a feat. What broke the contact was her inexperience concentrating, she guessed—and maybe the distraction of intense passion.

Pleased with herself, she grinned.

Knowing Mark, he's probably not surprised at what I did.

Within a blink, she felt kisses along her jaw and down her neck.

"Stop!" she hissed. "I'm at work!"

Alma heard him chuckle. She stopped herself from giggling then got her act together.

A thirst for knowledge overcame her. She wanted to learn fast; she needed to digest all the information passed on to her so she could get on with her new life.

I need to become proficient with these new powers as soon as possible.

My own safety and the security of the boys depend on me assimilating as much as possible and as quickly as my brain can absorb. But I still don't understand the total scope of things.

What powers do I possess?

Could I be dangerous to myself or others because of my inexperience?

Many questions nudged at her subconscious and only time would produce the answers.

Mark entered her mind.

You will become proficient. Stop second guessing yourself and give it time. I'll see you soon.

The morning flew by. She had accomplished quite a bit.

A light knock sounded on the opened door. Molly approached the desk with her message. "Ms. Weston, Mr. St. Claire is here. Shall I show him in?" her face was lit with happiness.

"Gee, is it lunch time already? Where has the morning gone?" she said. "Sure, Molly, show him in."

Minutes later Mark entered the room. Alma stood up and came around the desk and glided into his outstretched arms meeting his seeking lips.

They stood in the center of the room, door open for all to see, bodies molded together, savoring the kiss. When they finally broke apart, Alma's hands were still around Mark's neck, fingers toying with his blond hair.

"The purse was a big hit with my assistant, Mark. It's beautiful. Thank you so much," she stammered. "Whatever possessed you to buy such an expensive purse? Will I ever get to use it?"

He grinned. "It doesn't make any difference if you use it or not. I wanted to establish the fact you were marrying wealth and didn't need to work for a living. Did it work?"

"Molly was practically speechless—an incredible feat in and of itself. I'm sure everyone in the whole building knows about the Chloe purse, and that I'm leaving next Friday.

"She's been missing in action since this morning so I'm sure she's been wearing out her thumbs messaging everyone. Is Preston picking the boys up after school, or are you?"

"Preston will fetch them. They'll explore the house and grounds with Spencer and Preston. They'll learn a lot about me, the house, Kredo and many other things over the next few days. Spencer and Preston will think of things I may overlook—those simple, everyday things that make boys curious. There's no need to worry about them," he told her.

"I realize that. It's difficult for me to adjust. Will they finish up the school year?" She moved away from him. "Are we going out to lunch, or going home?"

"You're full of questions today, aren't you?" He laughed.

"It might look strange if the boys didn't go to school. Plus, they would run out of things to do staying home all day. There's only a couple of weeks until the summer break, and they need to learn the basics. Kredon education is different and I feel they can pursue that after their Earth education. Both systems have specific values, and education never hurts anyone."

"I hope they don't make any serious blunders, telling stories to their friends to show off, that kind of thing," Alma said, concerned.

"I doubt if they will. They have learned much more than you actually, and I think they take certain things for granted," Mark said.

"I guess I'm just skittish, waiting for an incident to crop up. I'm starving," she concluded.

"Our lunch reservations are at Tony's. Is that okay?"

"Tony's! I've never been inside the place. Everyone says it costs a fortune and none of my acquaintances have ever been there before," she said. "Am I dressed for the place?"

"Alma, you always look great; don't worry about it. Next time I'll keep it a secret," he joked.

"You will get used to this. It's your new way of life on Earth. I don't entertain at home very much, but I get invited to quite a few social and political functions, so you'll adjust.

"The rule is money opens doors and makes vain people trip over their feet to please you. They want to make sure they're seen with the richest people so they can name-drop later and get on all the right guest registers in town.

"When we go to Kredo it will be similar. There will be assemblies, committees, public speeches, galas, and so many other things I can't even remember them all. Remember, your father is the ruler and you will succeed him. This will be good experience for you. We need to get going."

Alma tilted her head in understanding. She went back to the desk and retrieved her purse out of the drawer.

"Do we have enough time to stop by my boss' office so I can introduce you?" she asked. "I promised I would show him who was taking me away from all of this." She swept her arms out around the room.

Ron had an appointment so the exchange of pleasantries was limited to a mild inquest, the opponents shaking hands, and calling a draw.

Alma sighed in relief as she shut the door. She glanced at Mark and rolled her eyes.

"Is that guy always this uptight?" Mark asked.

"What do you expect? He's been my boss for years and he knows the type of life I've led. This is a monumental shock for the poor man. Have some compassion!" They walked toward the elevator.

"I realize that, but he practically asked for my driver's license and Social Security card. There's such a thing as being overprotective." Mark was miffed.

"Don't worry about it, he's harmless. He won't run to the phone and call the Feds to check you out; he wants to make sure you're the real thing. Not many people care that much about others," she said.

"I understand. Yes, we owe him for his dedication. He stayed by you through a difficult time."

"By the way, do you have a driver's license and a Social Security card?" she joked.

"Don't be silly," he said, leaving her guessing.

Chapter 8

The group sat under a sprawling pecan tree and looked like two grandfathers and their grandsons enjoying each other's company, instead of four aliens discussing things that scientists only dreamed of and writers fantasized about.

Preston looked different out of uniform in his casual dress of khaki pants, a knit shirt, and a baseball cap. No one would guess he chauffeured a two-hundred-thousand-dollar car.

On the other hand, Spencer played the English butler to the tee. He wore precisely pressed black slacks, and a crisp white short-sleeved shirt.

Preston didn't think Spencer owned anything less than dress pants. He never wore jeans. His parted graying hair could withstand a breeze. Spencer had insisted on the blanket they sat on to protect his pants.

The discussion centered on their changing lives, the boys' heritage, and the undeveloped powers inside their minds as they snacked on finger sandwiches, apple slices and oatmeal cookies.

"You can't hold it against your mother, Cody," Preston was telling the eight-year-old. "She did not know of Mark until just a few weeks ago and then only in dreams. Many things were hidden from her as a protection. Like the old Earthling saying: what you don't know won't hurt you—that applies here. People would have come long ago to hurt your mother and to kidnap you two boys.

"Your mother will rule Kredo when your grandfather steps down from that position, and you will be your mother's successor, Cody. Asedi has been searching for her for many years. Now he knows where she is and has discovered you two, the situation is much more dangerous. Now we need to protect the two of you."

"Why did mom think Grandpa was dead? And how come she didn't think she was from Mars?" Jamie questioned.

"Do you feel any different, knowing your mother is from another world, Jamie?" Spencer asked. "You're not green with two heads or twelve arms—you appear and act just like everyone else on the planet."

"Perhaps we should show you the difference between Kredons and Earthlings." Preston projected a holographic vision of two internal male forms.

"Wow! How'd you do that?" Cody asked. The image captured their attention.

"You'll learn how to project images," Preston said. He tapped Cody on the head. "It's all in there."

"Wow! I can't wait to learn that," Cody said.

"As you can tell, there are no differences between these bodies from the neck down so let's get rid of the bodies and concentrate on the brains, shall we?"

Two large detailed pictures of brains appeared in midair, sectioned and labeled, easy to understand. Then, Preston projected a duplicate of himself into the hologram to point out the items they would talk about.

"Can you see any differences between these two pictures?" Spencer asked.

The boys studied in silence. "There's a couple of places in that brain that are bigger than in the other one." Cody pointed to the brain on the left.

"What's that blue line?" Jamie pointed. "The other brain doesn't have one of those."

"Superb observation," Preston commented. "Yes, Kredons have a thicker layer of cortex, where that blue line is, which might be compared to a highly sophisticated computer.

"The information your mother carried around, but wasn't aware of, is stored in her memory in the right hemisphere of her brain.

"These differences and others are important for you to understand because you will learn that these distinctions are why we can do so many more things than the people of this planet can."

"These holograms, for instance, and our abilities to get into other people's minds—our projections—are all a part of our complex brains.

"Earth will get to this point somewhere in time, but it won't be for quite a long while—maybe hundreds of years from now. Some have primitive abilities, but the entire human species has centuries to catch up to even the primitive Kredon level. Do you understand a little more now?" Preston asked.

"But what about Grandpa?" Jamie egged on. "Didn't he want to see Mom, or us?"

"Your grandfather thought it was best not to communicate with your mother because of the dangers involved. If they visited or sent messages, someone might have followed and told the bad people where to find your mother.

"No one knew what planet your mother lived on, except for a few selected, trusted friends, and it has taken years for the rebels to check all the places they suspected," Preston explained.

"Always remember this—sometimes you can't tell the good guys from the bad guys, like that mean old man looking inside your mind, Jamie," Preston said.

"He used to be one of the good guys. No one knows what causes a person to turn bad, and there aren't any warning signs or hints that are noticeable in an advanced society such as ours."

"Show us what Kredo looks like again," Cody begged.

Preston and Spencer drew on each other's powers and projected a combined view from their minds. The sky was greyish-blue with not one sunbeam in sight.

On a clear day, the features of the four moons could be seen from the surface of the planet. This vision was of an overcast day, making the moons seem ghostly on the horizon.

Craggy mountains stood majestic against the skyline, looking like huge stalagmites typically seen in caverns.

There was an immense amount of open country in the scene, like a desert. The reddish surface was almost devoid of vegetation, except for a few clumps of purplish foliage.

Kredo looked hot.

The sun in the Hozard solar system was twice the size of the Earth's sun, and Kredo was in the same position as Mars: fourth from the sun. It was larger than the planet Neptune, being forty-nine thousand nine hundred kilometers in diameter, and had an atmosphere almost identical to Alma's foster home, Earth, but with soaring temperatures.

The scene switched to a metropolitan area. Amid the parched soil and jagged mountains stood architecture unknown to Earth.

Buildings that looked like stacked doorknobs were common, and tall pyramid-spiked structures dotted the horizon. None looked like anything found in downtown Houston.

"Where do all the people live?" Cody asked. "There aren't very many buildings, and there are no houses. Don't you guys live in houses?"

"There are no individual homes such as the one you live in. Kredo has a population of only four hundred million people, and most of them live underground in complete freedom. There are networks of communities down there." Spencer chuckled at the question.

"Our standard of living is extremely comfortable compared to Earth. Families have separate living compartments, which are spacious and luxurious compared to the low and middle-income families you are familiar with, and our craftsmanship is far superior.

"You'll find thousands of topside cities where scientists live and work, such as the city shown here. There are around sixty buildings here in Kethlon, and these specific facilities monitor surface conditions, grow food, and purify water.

"Kredo looks like a desert, but underneath she's a virtual ocean. Our underground communities surround water. Unlike the people who live on the surface, we don't need to worry about water storms or any of the other surface hazards. There are traces of surface water all over the planet, but the majority is submerged.

"Do you see those domed buildings?" Spencer asked the boys.

They nodded.

"If you look closely, you'll see they are equipped with special solar panels. They are a little different from the solar panels you may have seen on some roofs here in Houston.

"Because Kredo is so close to her sun, our scientists had to develop special panels to screen the sun's rays so we could grow the plants below the surface. Otherwise the rays would burn everything in the special growing facilities," Spencer said.

"Is that why you all live underground?" Cody asked.

"No. Everyone lived on the surface until four centuries ago when industry was in full swing. We polluted the air and water to the point where we were killing ourselves. We had air alerts continuously, and on those days, no one could go outside. Harvests died, animals died, and thousands of people died. All in the name of progress.

"A great man named Gengora began the underground exodus with three buildings. One was for his family and friends, one was for their animals and the other was for growing plant-type foods similar to your fruits and vegetables, under artificial lighting.

"He had some problems along the way, as all pioneers do, but he succeeded, and thousands followed suit, escaping the air pollution," Spencer said.

"Gengora was a great architect," Preston added in admiration. "He designed those dome-shaped buildings hundreds of years ago, and they are considered the most efficient buildings. Gengora was ridiculed at first, but people saw the wisdom in his way of life."

"Wow!" Jamie pointed to the vision. "My brain went right inside that building! They're growing plants and things in there, Cody!"

Preston and Spencer glanced at each other in surprise, over the boys' heads.

"What else did you notice, Jamie?" Preston asked.

Thinking for several minutes, Jamie stared at the vision. "Each floor has different size plants, and that last floor was not as well-lit as the other floors."

"What do you see, Cody?" Spencer asked.

"They begin the seedlings on the top floor, where they filter out the sun's rays. Those plants on the first floor don't get any sunlight. What color is that? Green? I'll bet it's because they're going to go underground and they need to get used to the change in light, right?" the boy asked non-stop in his inquisitiveness.

"How do you think you saw all of that?" Preston asked the boys.

"I kind of took my brain and eyes over there," Jamie said.

"That was really neat. It was like looking through the air!" Cody exclaimed.

"You're both learning fast, but it will take a lot of work. You can practice on things around you, but I must warn you, do not poke into someone's mind, just to eavesdrop. Kredons don't do that. We believe in privacy above all else. So, don't embarrass yourselves or others by doing that," Spencer said.

Both boys nodded.

"How come Kredo doesn't have as many people as Earth?" Cody asked. "They said on the news we had over seven billion people, and it's a lot smaller than Kredo."

"If Gengora hadn't shown us how to live underground, there would be fewer of us than there are now," Preston said.

"People and animals were succumbing from the poisoned air. We learned a valuable lesson: respect nature. When nature warns, you'd better pay attention. We didn't hundreds of years ago, but we sure listen and follow instructions now."

"Are there wars there like there are here?" Jamie asked.

"No, not really. The planet is unified. What caused the revolution was a lunatic named Asedi lusting for power. He was greedy and couldn't get enough wealth. He built his army with hardened criminals, most of whom were willing to go along with anything just to get off Ecko, the prison moon," Spencer said.

"You see, the prisoners could not use their mind powers anymore. The law states that offenders have a tiny disc implanted inside their temporal lobes in the brain, which renders them powerless. Anyone who joined Asedi in the revolution had the implant removed."

Preston pointed to the area of the hologram. As the conversation changed, the hologram vanished, changing the school scene back to blue sky once again.

Not accustomed to luxury, Alma marveled at the exclusive setting of Tony's. From the minute they arrived at the front door, they were attended to and pampered like royalty, beginning with the valet parking.

The maître d' greeted Mark as he escorted Alma through the beautiful beveled glass front door.

Alma's eyes were as big as oceans trying to see everything at once. The staff bustled about their business in the crowded room.

The minute they were seated, two members of the staff approached. One poured the water, the other seemed eager to see to their needs.

Mark ordered a bottle of wine.

Only half listening to the exchange of words, Alma was busy taking in her surroundings. She was fascinated that she could see the hive of activity in the kitchen.

The waiter returned with the wine Mark had chosen and poured the red liquid into the wine glasses.

"Are you ready to order?" the waiter asked.

"Yes. Start us with your seafood gumbo, then the Wyatt salad," Mark said.

"You look lovely in this setting, Alma," Mark said, seductively.

"This place is wonderful! The people who work here appear so content. It's a nice, comfortable feeling to be waited on by people who like what they're doing," she said.

The waiter returned with the gumbo. Alma dipped her spoon into the bowl and tasted. "Oh, this is fabulous!"

"I'm glad you like it. Tony's gumbo is my favorite in the city," Mark said.

Another waiter, passing by, replenished the wine in their glasses.

"Your mind is in a million places, isn't it?"

"I've never had the opportunity to come to this upscale of a restaurant before. It's wonderful. I can understand how someone could get used to this type of treatment."

"There's no going back, you know." Mark slipped inside her mind and caressed her ever so softly.

Alma turned her head toward him and returned his caress. It lasted only a second, but she had slipped inside his mind, brushed her hand against his cheek then turned his hand, palm up and lightly kissed its center before slipping out again.

"You need to learn how to concentrate deep inside your mind and still look alert on the outside for the rest of the world to ignore. Find something interesting to focus on, Alma. Now, let's experiment. Come to me," he demanded.

His sexy voice excited her. She watched the kitchen hustle and bustle through the glass wall and concentrated on Mark, placing herself in back of his chair and putting her arms around his neck. She glanced up at her visible body across the table and was satisfied that she looked normal staring at the kitchen.

Alma experimented with making her physical eyes glance around the room. She nipped Mark's ear and rejoined her counterpart. She smiled wickedly and winked at him.

"You're doing well. A little more practice and you'll be a real pro. Never forget that you must appear natural. You don't want anyone to suspect there is anything remotely out of place. I know this sounds ludicrous, but you have to practice being in two places at one time. And while you are, you must learn how to converse while your other self is wandering around.

"You don't want people to think you're slipping into a coma or something equally weird like a trance. Here comes the waiter. Watch closely," he said with confidence.

"Your Wyatt salads, Mr. St. Claire. Can I get you anything else?" the man asked.

"This should be sufficient," he said. ["See how easy it is, Alma?" he whispered in her ear as his fingers brushed her nipple.]

Alma had a difficult time controlling her surprise with his little demonstration.

"Excellent, sir. I'll be back soon to check on you."

Tony Vallone stopped by their table. If she hadn't known any better, Alma would have assumed the two were best of friends.

"Mark, good to see you," Tony said.

Mark stood. He and Tony shook hands.

"May I present Alma Weston?" Mark said.

Tony shook Alma's hand. "How nice to meet you. Is this your first visit to my restaurant?"

"Yes. I'm thoroughly enjoying the experience. It's nice to see what's going on in the kitchen," Alma said.

Tony said his goodbyes and moved on.

"Don't you ever do that again, Mark!" she exclaimed in a whisper. "I almost jumped out of my chair!"

"You could have fooled me. On the outside, you looked cool and collected." He laughed.

"I can see I'll have my hands full with you!" she said. "Don't play tricks on me, Mark. Never take advantage of me!"

"No tricks, but I would like to take advantage of you right now," he said.

"Well, behave or you'll be prying me off the ceiling."

Mark shook his head in denial, he smiled knowingly.

Chapter 9

U pon finishing their meal, Alma looked like a contented cat. Taking another sip of wine, she faced
Mark. "I've never had such a fantastic meal in my life.
People must spend hours here at suppertime. Thank you so
very much for bringing me here."

"You're more than welcome," he said. "We will come
again."

A waiter set a payment tray on the table and left. Mark
dropped two bills on the tray. Shocked, she stared at the tray
as Mark stood and helped her up.

"Aren't you going to get change?" she whispered.

"No. That covers our meal and a tip," Mark replied.

"Two hundred dollars for lunch? My God! That's what I
spend on groceries every two weeks! You've got to be kidding!"

"Alma I know this is all new to you, but this was a cheap
meal compared to others in this room. Believe me." He
smiled. "Don't worry, Alma. I'll take care of you and teach
you."

"I have so much to learn. Everything you take for granted
is new to me. I've had to work for a living and never had

luxuries. People would be shocked to know my father is the ruler of a world larger than the Earth."

"It will all come naturally. I promise," Mark said. "I know it seems impossible right now, but you have to give it a little time. Before you know it, you will be more aware of your powers and you will be able to use them efficiently. You will become comfortable in any setting. It just takes time."

As he finished speaking, the attendant drove the shiny red Ferrari sedately to the curb where Mark and Alma waited.

The valet held the door for Mark. He took Alma's arm and escorted her to the other side of the car and handed her inside, locking and closing the door after her.

He smiled and saluted as Mark drove off, happy with the generous tip.

After a few zigs and zags in and out of traffic, Memorial Drive loomed ahead. Mark drove slightly over the speed limit and maneuvered the car down the busy street. He turned into the driveway of the building where Alma worked

"I don't have that much to do today so I think I'm going to leave early. Won't that shock them on top of everything else?" Alma chuckled.

Mark helped Alma out of the car; they walked toward the building. The lobby was practically deserted; the friendly face of John, the security guard smiled at them as they entered the building.

"Afternoon Ms. Weston, Mr. St. Claire. Nice day today," he said.

"Yes, it is a lovely day. I'm leaving early today, John, so I'll be back down in a few minutes," she said.

"This is the perfect day to take off. Go to the park and relax," the older man said.

The elevator doors glided open and Mark pushed the button for the fifth floor. The elevator rides were becoming remarkably smoother with each passing day. It amazed her. Within minutes, they reached their destination, left the confined space and headed toward her office.

They breezed past Molly, who was munching a sandwich while watching a YouTube video. Alma entered her office with Mark on her heels.

The beautiful purse was where she had left it hours ago. Alma wondered how many hands had examined it since she had left for lunch. An efficient person, her desk was tidy, so there was nothing for her to do except lock up.

Mark picked up the box, replaced the top cover and waited for Alma while she shut down her computer. She waved Mark ahead of her while she took one more glance around the room.

Alma turned off the overhead light and closed the door. They paused at Molly's desk, and Alma informed her that she was leaving for the day.

"I'll tell Ron that you've left early. Have a nice afternoon." Her boss never left early unless one of the kids was sick. She wasn't turning over a new leaf; she was growing a whole new tree!

It felt like she was playing hooky and Alma was jubilant to leave early. "This is wonderful!" she said, dancing around Mark as they left the building. Stopping in front of him, she stood on tiptoes and kissed him.

He drew her to him with his free arm and deepened the kiss. Heat radiated from his body. Each time she made physical contact with him, it was like a forest fire; the blaze spread quickly through her limbs.

Alma groaned from the ecstasy he was wracking her with. She pried her mind away from his sensual assault. She opened her eyes and met his blue wells that were glazed with passion.

A scene unfolded before her: tangled bodies on his enormous bed. His powers were strong, and she didn't know how to fight him off yet. Did she really want to? She answered her own question in less than a second: No! She wanted this forever.

"I think we'd better get going before we make a spectacle of ourselves, or get arrested," he whispered in her ear.

Shaking her head in dazed agreement, Alma let him lead her to the car. Tossing the box in the back compartment, he got in behind the wheel and drove home.

Changing into a brown and gold flowing sun dress, Alma padded around in her bare feet. Mark had placed the box on the dressing table and had left the house to attend to business.

Walking through the connecting door to her sitting room, Alma glanced around. No books were in sight. She left the room and wandered down the hallway.

She peeked into Cody's room, then Jamie's room. Both were empty. The place was a virtual tomb, so silent.

Alma decided to search the library for something worth reading. She continued down the hall and walked silently down the beautiful, wide stairs.

Spencer and Preston must be with the boys.

Where has Mark disappeared to?

Changing course, she headed to the kitchen to see if Cook was around. As she came closer to the kitchen, she heard the familiar noises of the cook in the process of creating one of her wonderful marvels.

Alma walked through the open doorway and smiled.

Cook stood at one of the many counters in her billowy white apron with smudges of flour on her face and hands.

Upon seeing Alma, she rushed over, wiping her hands on the floury apron.

"Why hello, missy. Can I get you a nice cup of tea?" the cheerful, rotund woman asked.

"That would be terrific," Alma said. "I assumed I was the only one in the house. It gets so quiet in here sometimes."

"You need to practice. While you're listening, you must learn to scan with your senses so you can detect danger," Cook said, matter-of-factly.

"Learn to expand your mind and see inside and through things. Danger can lurk any place. Learn to look into the walls and through a sunbeam. Train yourself to be sensitive."

Listening and nodding, Alma knew this was good advice. "I hope I can learn everything quicker than the way it's coming to me." She frowned.

"Don't you fret now. It will take time, but you'll be surprised—when you need that power of yours, it will be there and you will know what to do with it. Sometimes it just takes an emergency to wade through all the lessons. Here's some nice hot tea."

"Just the way I like it." Alma smiled at the jovial woman. "I think I'll take this into the library. I want to find something to read."

"Try the green bound books with the gold lettering. They look like English classics but are actually Kredon history books. I think you'll find them fascinating," Cook said.

"I hate to sound so stupid, but do you have a real name?" Alma asked.

"Oh, my dear. I've been called Cook for so long that I wouldn't answer to my given name. But between you and me, my name's really Gwever. I come from a long line of cooks, and my family's the best in a kitchen on either planet!"

"What a beautiful name! Would you mind, when we're alone, if I call you that? It'll be our secret," Alma said, earnestly.

"That would be lovely. Now run along to the library and I'll make sure we don't starve tonight." Gwever was pleased at the sincere friendliness of the new mistress.

Balancing the cup of tea on the saucer, Alma went to the library. She glanced around for the green bound books and spotted them on a top shelf.

She slid the library ladder along the top railing then pushed the rubber stop down to keep the ladder from moving. She climbed the rungs to the sixth section.

Twelve beautiful bound volumes completed the set.

I'll start at the beginning and work my way through the series.

Wondering what else was hidden away, she glanced across the rows and rows of bound books before climbing down.

The room was immense.

There must be thousands of books here.

Alma flipped through the pages of the heavy tome in her hands. She walked toward the inviting leather sofa, similar to the one in Mark's sitting room and sat down. Alma curled her feet under her.

The contents mystified her. Unknown words stared back at her probing eyes. Pages and pages of neat script, charts, maps, and drawings were contained in the book. Carefully turning the pages, she concentrated deeply.

Slowly, as a reel of film turning to life, the words became discernible.

Reading in silence for several minutes, she stopped to digest the history the volume contained. Kredo was millions of years older than Earth.

No wonder the civilization was much more advanced. Earth was in baby stages compared to the scientific knowledge that she read in the book on her lap.

How much knowledge have I gotten from the few pages I've read? How much information have I unknowingly pulled from the depths of my mind?

The concept intrigued her. Alma stared into the middle of the room, balancing her thoughts. She decided that the hidden knowledge inside her mind was unraveling little by little.

Flipping through several more pages, she stopped at an interesting section that discussed the four moons.

As she read intently, the feeling that someone was watching her swept over her. She looked up to a wavering apparition of a strange group of people.

Three of the visitors wore gray cloaks; three wore blue fitted clothing similar to jumpsuits. The group stood silently observing her, she sat staring in return.

Knowing instinctively that she was not in any danger, Alma sat transfixed on the sofa unable to pull her eyes away from the people before her. They fascinated her.

The only Kredons she knew were Mark and the staff, and they all dressed and talked like Earthlings. This experience was totally exhilarating.

"Do you wish to ask me something?" she asked the group. Shocked, she realized that she had spoken Kredon.

The room remained silent. Worry filtered down to her subconscious. Without realizing what she was doing, she encompassed herself in a protective shield and encircled the group with a mind bubble.

Their mind chatter filled the room with a riot of noise. She felt as if she had been caught eavesdropping because they were busy assessing her and were surprised that she had detected them.

From what she gathered from the conversations, they should have been invisible to her eyes. Her development was going well. They would have much to report to Jetron when they returned to Cralic Sector.

Cook heard the commotion in the relatively quiet kitchen and stopped what she was doing. She wiped her dusty floured hands on her apron and crept cautiously down the hall to the library. Stopping outside the closed door, she projected herself to the other side, into the room.

Quietly assessing the situation, she approached the group, keeping her distance from Alma's mind probe. She knew the mistress couldn't see her, but the delegation could.

"She is learning fast. It was foolish for you to come here. She is much more advanced than her father suspected. Some Earth culture and training gets in the way at times.

"Poor dear, but when a part of her Kredon heritage filters through her mind, she grasps it immediately. There's no need for her to repeat a lesson. Go quickly before she probes deeper," Cook warned, leaving the room.

After a few minutes of standing silently, as if listening to someone else, the wavering images vanished, leaving the room silent again.

Not hearing or seeing anything else, Alma wondered about that silence. She felt a sense of approval from the group; she removed her protective shield and hoped that her heart rate would slow to normal.

Yes, she was learning, even though she hadn't realized it before. From some hidden place inside her she had known automatically what to do, how to do it, and why she should take the action she did.

What is buried in my brain?

A language, a culture, knowledge that had not been there last week was bubbling over, waiting to emerge. She felt frustrated. Certain things were happening too fast, and other things were taking too long for her to understand.

Maybe if I could open my head and stuff those twelve green bound books inside, the answers would be instantaneous.

What will my father say when the group reports their findings? Will he come to visit me?

Secrecy was no longer necessary as far as she was concerned. Asedi already knew where she was.

Sitting quietly on the sofa, she remembered Gwever's words. Letting her mind wander free, she cleared out the chatter and felt the empty space in the room.

The remnants of emotions and conversations clung to objects. A ficus tree shed its leaves, upset from harsh words.

Plants and natural materials, she discovered, were greatly affected by moods. Plants required not only water and light, but a soothing environment.

Wood, metal, rock, and other natural objects would dry out, pit, rust, corrode—just to name a few symptoms—if they absorbed an argument, hate, or deceit.

Alma picked up mixed feelings from all the objects in the room and sent a wave of love energy to be distributed to each object. She was instantly rewarded with a cozy warmth, her thank-you from the many natural materials.

Chapter 10

The remaining time at work sped by quickly. Surprisingly, no emergencies cropped up. She dug through her desk drawers and removed personal items and placed them in a box, along with photos and her coffee cup.

The remainder of the time had been spent wisely—updating all personnel files and noting important dates in her tickler file. Next, she boxed up old paper files and had Molly arrange for them to be stored off-site for safekeeping.

All was in order. The new person would be able to come in, sit down at the immaculately arranged desk, and take over.

Ron had begun interviewing candidates starting in-house in hopes of replacing Alma. Only two in-house candidates applied, but neither had all the right qualifications.

After many conversations, Alma finally convinced her boss to upgrade the position, changing the title and salary grade.

An assigned parking place was not enough incentive for the job, she argued. A professional wanted a title and salary that looked good on a resume.

After rewriting the job description, Alma sent copies to all the online job boards. It was only a matter of time before the right person would come along.

Dedicated to her profession, she would never consider leaving the place in a mess. She documented everything she could think of in the job descriptions including Molly's duties.

Alma sealed the detailed instructions in a private envelope then placed a smaller envelope in the center of the desk. She stuck a sticky note with instructions for the new person to remind Ron to hand over the large envelope.

With no one around, anyone would be able to slip inside the office and shut the door. She didn't want to take a chance that the larger envelope would be accidentally thrown out or peeked at.

Not understanding the baser instincts of some people, Molly was too naïve and believed only in the good in people.

Unfortunately, Alma knew otherwise and felt that it was her duty to protect the company from any mischief. Her desk and files would remain locked and Ron would have the keys.

Friday. After what seemed like a two-hundred-hour week, her last day at Hunter and Bloomfield finally arrived. She had been on edge all week, waiting for the day.

A never-ending procession of people stopped by her office to wish her luck. Even Mr. Macho, Doug Harris, dropped by.

"I wanted to wish you well, Alma," he said squirming.

His confession would follow and she decided to play with it.

"I'm sorry for the trouble I caused you; I've really been an ass."

"Doug, I appreciate your owning up about that. It would have been nice to be friends with you but I decided it would be inappropriate since we worked together.

"In corporate life, friendships are often mistaken for affairs and cause a lot of grief. I'm sure if you had asked again, instead of beginning your verbal attack, I would have gone to lunch or dinner with you. See what you did? Keep that in mind for future reference."

I hope my nose doesn't grow two feet or my tongue fall off for this outrageous lie!

A large group was taking her to lunch at her favorite Italian restaurant.

She suspected very little work would get done when they returned.

I hope they all pay their share and don't leave poor Ron to cough up the rest of the cash.

People didn't think about the sales tax or the tip.

Molly and Ron showed up at her office promptly at eleven-thirty.

"Well, kid, are you ready?" Ron asked.

This is so difficult for him. Who am I kidding? It's hard for me too!

She and Ron had worked side by side for so long. She would miss his gentle and caring friendship, his fatherly advice and the easy rapport from the years of working together.

"Is it that time already?"

They left her office in silence.

Of course, the elevator's creaking again.

As the doors slid open, Alma spied a tear in Molly's eye.

"Don't you dare cry, Molly Jenkins!" Alma scolded, hoping to stop the rush of tears that would come.

An emotional person, Molly cried every time someone left, had a baby, or got married.

Alma placed her arm around Molly's shoulder. "It's okay, Molly, I'm just teasing. You can cry all you want. It wouldn't be the same if you didn't."

"Oh, Ms. Weston, I can't believe you're leaving," Molly said, blubbering. "It won't be the same here without you. What if the new person doesn't like me, or if I don't like her? I'll have to find another job and there aren't that many jobs available right now."

Ron came to the rescue with a pat on the back and a small tissue pack.

Molly dabbed at her eyes. Red-faced, mascara a mess, she continued crying and dabbing at her eyes.

Ron smiled. *She's so young.* "You're not going to have to quit your job, Molly. I'm the boss, remember? Don't worry; everything will work out and you'll get along fine with the new person, whenever we find someone as brilliant as Alma, that is," he teased.

"Are you sure, Mr. Finkley?" Molly asked. "People can be pretty sneaky when they don't like someone."

"You'll get to meet everyone I interview, Molly," he said. "I'll even let them sit out front by you for about ten minutes so you can talk to each person. If you don't like someone, you just tell me when they've left."

"Okay, Mr. Finkley." Molly brightened. "That would work out just fine."

Molly beamed, exited the cranky elevator at the lobby level, calm and tearless.

After two hours of eating and toasting each other, everyone was stuffed to satisfaction when they finally left the restaurant. Beer and wine had flowed freely, and garlic bread never ran out.

Alma had a difficult decision to make while studying the menu. She finally ordered her favorite dish, lasagna. Everyone agreed that Italian food was too good to have only one favorite.

Her loving coworkers had presented her with a stunning gift: A beautiful Waterford wine decanter. Alma was moved with emotion at the presentation and almost broke her resolve not to cry.

The trip back to work was fairly quick.

Molly cried.

"She's practicing for the wedding tomorrow," Ron told Alma, smiling.

"She couldn't possibly have one tear left for tomorrow," Alma joked.

Molly dabbed her red, swollen eyes with a rumpled, wet tissue, sniffed and remained silent, trying to control herself.

They rode the elevator in silence, and Molly scooted out the doors and rushed to the restroom to repair the damage to her makeup. No doubt she would be horrified when she saw the destruction, Alma thought affectionately.

Minutes later, Mark stepped out of the elevator. He strode up to Alma, kissed her, then placed his arm around her shoulders.

"I made a map for your boss and Molly so they won't get lost tomorrow. Are you all set to go?" he asked.

"Yes. Let me go and make a copy of this and I'll give them each their own map. Molly has been crying all day, so don't pay close attention to her eyes when you see her," Alma said. She didn't want Molly to be embarrassed more than she was. "I'll be right back."

Mark waited in the tidy office and looked around; Alma's presence was still strong in the quiet room. Her essence would remain for weeks—that he was sure of.

When she returned to her office, Alma smiled up at him and met his lips halfway in a quick kiss, before retrieving her purse from the cleared desk. With a quick glance around, she left the memories behind and headed out the door with Mark carrying her box.

They walked past Molly's empty desk; Alma smiled and shook her head. "Heavens! I've never seen anyone cry so much in my life. Tomorrow should prove to be disastrous for Molly. Remind me to buy a cold pack for her eyes. She's going to need it," Alma said.

The elevator appeared in seconds after Mark punched the down button and Alma noted that it was quicker this time than the first experience. Somewhere in the back of her mind she had the idea that their combined energy was the explanation.

How can I put it to a test?

The trip down to street level was quiet while she pondered over the idea, with no solution in mind. She'd keep that on the back burner and would come up with something, eventually.

Except for occasional small talk, Mark left Alma to dwell on her private musings, not probing her secrets during the short ride home.

At times, he seemed to understand her better than she knew herself. Right now, he suspected she was putting the past away and preparing for the future. When they pulled up to the front of their elegant home, Jamie and Cody came bounding up to the sleek Ferrari.

"Wait until you see the gardens, Mom!" Cody squealed.

"We helped Preston and Spencer with decorations. It's beautiful!" Jamie yelled. "Are you going to come and see it now?"

"Let your mother change her clothes first so she can be comfortable," Mark told the two boys. "Why don't you go ask Cook to send a snack out back and we'll have a little party?"

Excited with that idea, the boys ran off to the side door that led directly to the kitchen.

"You're so good with them. I only wish that you had been around when they were born. How wonderful life would have been as a family; they would have had their real father who understood them. We could have been so happy." The wistful sadness in her eyes told him a lot.

"I can't do anything about the past. I can only promise you that our future is aligned where we are concerned. I'm not going away—ever. What we have is permanent and no matter where you go in the universe or beyond, my love for you will always be there. Never forget that," he said.

The efficient Spencer met them at the door. Alma handed the wine decanter to him. "I don't know where to put this."

"And did Miss Molly cry her eyes out?" the older man asked.

"Spencer, you don't surprise me for a minute. You keep track of everything!" Alma said. "I've never seen anyone cry so much!"

"Perhaps Miss Molly should take a vacation," the older man said.

Alma slipped inside his mind and kissed Spencer's cheek, making a blush come and go. "I don't know what I'd do without you, Spencer. Thank you for being you," she whispered.

Alma noticed a slight smile on Spencer's regal face; she could tell he was pleased as he headed off toward the rear of the house.

"You're going to have him eating out of your hand, Alma. Then I won't be able to boss him around." Mark joked as they climbed the stairs to the second floor, arm in arm.

Knowing the boys were waiting to show her the decorated yard for the wedding, she hurried and changed clothes. For a reason that was unknown to her, she was not nervous in the least.

Huh. No last-minute jitters, no sleepless nights.

Everything had happened so fast that there wasn't time to think or worry.

These past two weeks have changed me in more ways than one.

In this short time period, she had discovered who she was, although she had considered she had known herself so well before; she enjoyed getting to know the man who had changed her life so drastically.

As the days passed, she was becoming increasingly aware of the powers within her. It would take time to learn everything, but as she discovered, things seemed to unfold in her mind overnight. New knowledge came to the surface for her to experiment with.

After changing into shorts and a pullover, Alma went to inspect the gardens. What she saw left her overwhelmed.

"Oh, Mark, it's beautiful!"

Chains of white flowers were draped everywhere, and Chinese lanterns bobbed in the soft breeze. A dozen tables—all of them draped in white—with wooden folding chairs were ready for the guests.

"Thank you, boys!" She hugged them. "Thank you, Preston and Spencer!"

The two men beamed smiles as brilliant as the two boys. As promised, Cook brought a plate of finger sandwiches and a pitcher of lemonade.

Morning shown through the lacy curtains with sunlight peeping at Alma's eyes. Reluctantly, she opened them and directed her gaze toward the brilliant windows.

She reached out and discovered Mark's side of the bed was empty. She felt a sudden pang of loneliness. Alma glanced at the clock on the side table and was dismayed at the time.

Eleven o'clock! I've never slept so late in my life! Of all days!

She leapt out of bed and headed straight for the shower. The Justice of the Peace would arrive at one-thirty, then guests would start showing up around two.

The brisk water felt good on her skin, washing the cobwebs out of her head. She finished up, shut off the water and clutched one of the fluffy towels and wrapped her hair in a turban.

A vision of loveliness awaited in the dressing room.

OMG!

When she saw it, she had to sit. There was her wedding dress. A beautiful organza dress invited her to try it on. White with pale russet and lilac flowers, the full-length, sleeveless dress had a pleated neckline, and a dropped vee waist. The back of the skirt was gathered at the hem similar to Austrian curtains.

She hugged the dress to her and whirled around the room like a little girl. Alma took control of her giddiness and hung the dress back on the hook and started to get ready.

Now that she thought of it, she wondered if Mark had put one of his *don't worry about it* whispers in her mind. Up until this moment she couldn't imagine what she had planned to wear for the occasion.

After blow drying her hair, she applied a light amount of makeup, then began dressing. The white satin shoes she found on the shoe rack were perfect to tie the outfit together.

As she slipped the dress over her head, she smoothed it down on her body. It fit to perfection and looked divine on her figure. She stepped into the shoes and twirled once to see her full image in the mirror then left the room to find her family.

Twelve forty-five.

A soft delicate breeze fanned her dress lightly.

Ooh! It's a perfect day—not too hot, not too humid.
As she meandered in between the tables, she admired the setting. The tables were beautifully arranged with white tablecloths, a delicate lily-of-the-valley china pattern, fine crystal stemware, and a beautiful set of silverware.

Alma looked closer, and noticed, to her delight, that the tablecloth and napkins had lily-of-the-valley flowers embroidered on the edges and in the center.

That Gwever!

Each table held a small floral centerpiece.

The boys stood under the rose-covered arbor, dressed in their Sunday best.

They must be up to something.

They were so deep in conversation they didn't even hear her approach.

"You two look so serious. Are you plotting the downfall of the government?"

"Oh, we were just talking about Kredo. I can't wait to go there, Mom," Cody confided.

"Me, too!" Jamie piped up. "I want to see the buildings where they grow things, and the underground oceans."

"You've been learning a lot from Preston and Spencer, haven't you?" she asked. "That's good. I want you two to be knowledgeable about my birthplace. I have a lot to learn about it, as well."

"Are you going to be the queen, Mom?" Jamie asked.

"I guess you could just call me the ruler. There are no kings and queens on Kredo. Cody will inherit my place when

I get too old to do my job. You won't feel left out, will you, Jamie?"

The situation had bothered her: *the first born inherited. What about the other children if there were more than one?*

"Heck no. We've already talked about it. I'm going to be an advisor," the young boy said, in all seriousness.

"You'll make a wonderful advisor, Jamie," Alma said.

She was glad that the transition was easier for them. Because their father had been with them in his mysterious way, educating them even as babies, he poured his love and knowledge into them.

It must have been painful for Mark not to be able to share in the births. Not to be able to physically, in person, hold each of the boys when they were born and then having to silently stand by and watch someone else, an outsider, take those precious rights away from him.

Especially when that person never shared a great interest in parenting. It had been a strange relationship with Jeff.

Mark caught a glimpse of his family and strolled across the manicured lawn to join them. He looked magnificent in his impeccably tailored cream-colored tux and color-coordinated shirt and tie. Alma noted that the shirt was off-white and blended in well; his cream-colored shoes were an exact match to the suit.

Where does he find all the coordinating clothes?

His blue eyes looked stunning, the same color as the brilliant sky overhead. Captured by his charisma, Alma longed to run her fingers through his blond hair.

He affected her the same way every time she saw him—a powerful undercurrent of desire rumbled through her body, waiting to explode. She wanted to make love to him, staring into those blue eyes.

Alma was thrilled knowing his feelings ran as deep as hers. Their desire was mutual. There could be nothing worse than a one-way relationship. It wasn't just sex—there were deep feelings she had never experienced before. Comfort, trust, sharing. A satisfaction that all areas in her life were fulfilled, finally.

"You look wonderful." He looked deep within her eyes to her inner self. "Are you nervous?"

"No, surprisingly, I'm not."

"I'd like to show you something." He reached into his pants pocket. Mark pulled out a small velvet bag and opened the braided strings. Two intricately designed gold bands sparkled in the sunlight, each snugly nestled in place with a velvet loop of material.

"Mark, they're lovely!" she exclaimed, touching the precious metal.

"They're examples of Kredon craftsmanship," Mark said proudly. He glanced toward the house and noticed a visitor. "There's Mr. Antonelli, the violinist. Come and meet him, Alma. Boys, stay out of trouble and try not to get too grubby before people get here."

"Don't worry, dad, we won't climb any trees right now." When his parents were out of earshot, Cody whispered to his brother, "We'll wait until everyone is busy!"

"Oh, no, you won't. You can spare one day for your parents and be on your best behavior." Mark's voice boomed inside their minds.

Mark chuckled as he watched their shocked expressions; he had caught them off-guard.

It will do them good to remember the powers of the mind. I'll have to keep those two on their toes.

"Peter!" Mark clasped his friend's hand and introduced Alma.

How does Mark know a concert violinist?

Alma marveled at the many people he seemed to be acquainted with.

He's into everything—or is he? Does he plant suggestions into their minds of long time friendships along with memories?

The violinist settled in and began playing.

Oh, the guests are going to be so delighted!

The Justice of the Peace arrived, another of Mark's many acquaintances. Since the arrangements had been made so quickly, there hadn't been time for rehearsals. Alma was convinced there wasn't a need for any since the ceremony was going to be a simple affair.

They covered the details quickly and easily now, discussing where they were going to stand, the double rings, then chatted for a few minutes. One by one, and in pairs, the guests arrived.

Alma spotted Ron and Molly mingling with the guests, and she made her way across the lawn.

"You look terrific, Ms. Weston!" Molly chimed.

"Do you think you could try calling me Alma for the day, or you'll have to get used to St. Claire in a little while," Alma joked.

She hugged Molly affectionately. "I'm glad you both made it."

She scanned the lawn looking through the sea of people for another familiar face.

Mark didn't tell me there would be so many guests! I've counted at least forty-five, maybe more.

The long-awaited hour approached. The guests sat at the lovely tables while Alma and Mark took their places in front of the Justice of the Peace, with the two boys close by.

The soft strings of the violin made an enchanting atmosphere, then all was silent as the ceremony began.

How did Mark arrange everything so perfectly? It's just as well. I'm supposed to be an orphan.

Her mind drifted from the JP's droning voice. Alma let her eyes roam freely, without turning her head. As she glanced about, a wavering motion caught her eyes. She stared at it, a phenomenon similar to rising heat off a road in the summer. The wavering finally took form.

I wish I could turn to see the guests.

Her eyes flew to the JP then back to the spot where the Kredon delegation stood.

I know the guests can't detect them, but I wonder if Mark and the staff know they're here. And what about the boys? If Jamie and Cody have seen them, they're being awfully good.

As she stared at them, the group exchanged words and nodded. Evidently, they would return to her homeland and report on the ceremony.

Alma forced her mind back to the JP in front of her, lest she slip up and say "no" instead of "yes."

They approve. Mark slipped in and out of her mind.

Vows and rings were exchanged, kisses shared. The boys clapped as if they were at the circus. The delegation was still present.

How long do they intend to stay?

Minutes later, as if they had heard Alma's thoughts, they vanished.

Chapter 11

Everyone agreed that Cook outdid herself. The scrumptious buffet stretched across two long tables and offered everything from a crab-chunk salad, smoked salmon, and stuffed mushrooms, to red snapper Pontchartrain, and crepe Suzettes.

The cake was a five-tiered wonder with white frosting ribbons and bows atop butter cream frosting, a truly remarkable work of art. Two plastic figures, with radiant smiles etched on their tiny faces looked like the bride and groom.

Guests who noticed the similarity asked if the faces were hand-painted.

Flustered from all the attention, Cook explained that she bought them at a local dollar store; any similarities were a coincidence.

Alma recognized the twinkle of innocence on Cook's face and investigated the subjects of everyone's curiosity.

She stooped down and peered into the plastic faces. She raised an eyebrow and glanced over at a suddenly busy Cook.

As Alma engaged herself in a conversation with a guest, she split away from herself and zoomed to Cook's side.

"Gwever, you sly devil, what did you do to those dolls?" Alma asked.

Projecting an image of herself Cook split apart from her physical self with an innocent expression of "who me?" forming on her face, making Alma giggle.

"Why, Missy, all I did was to encourage their little faces with pin-pointed energy," Cook said. "Aren't they cute? All these women will go running to the store buying up dolls."

"Just think, when we go back to Kredo, we can tell everyone you started a new fad." Alma winked, then zipped back to her body.

Cook snickered over the comment and waved her hand, dismissing the idea, then merged back into one form.

Champagne flowed freely.

Molly drank and cried.

Alma glanced at Molly.

I'm sure she's having a good time, but it's hard to tell when her emotions are so on display. Good thing she'll have tomorrow to recuperate. Those eyes would take more than a few slices of cucumber, or tea bags to get back to normal.

Oddly enough, the crowd was more interested in conversing and imbibing than in dancing.

Since they weren't going on a honeymoon, Alma and Mark agreed that she would remain with the guests and not change into day clothes.

The boys plotted and played, and even mingled with the guests, telling their stories about dog bites, school and the daycare center. The dog bite story and the friend's pregnant mother story were competing for first place when Mark stopped counting.

Time sped by. One by one, the guests departed. By eight-thirty, the house and gardens were quiet once more.

"Boy, did you see how drunk Mr. Fipper was?" Cody asked Mark, giggling.

"I sure did. He was beyond tipsy, wasn't he," Mark replied. "I'm surprised you two didn't go off and hide somewhere. Weren't you bored with this?"

"We wanted to see everything. Wasn't the food great?" Jamie asked, trying to stifle a yawn.

"Yes, Cook is a marvel, isn't she? It's time for you two to get to bed. You've been up since early morning and you both have been really busy today. Don't worry, the food will still be here tomorrow," Alma told her sons.

"Can we have champagne tomorrow?" Jamie asked. His eyes were wide with hope.

"Add ten years to your birthdays, and you'd still be under-age." Mark smiled at his mischievous son.

"Okay," both boys chorused as they ran up the stairs to their bedrooms.

"My feet ache." Alma sank down on the sofa and slipped her shoes off. "I'm so glad today is behind us. I don't think I can do that again!"

"You're never going to get that chance again," Mark replied playfully. "You're stuck with me, Alma."

Mark leaned over and planted a loud, wet kiss on the side of her mouth.

"I need to get into something loose and comfortable before I scream," Alma said. "I'll be back in a minute."

Alma climbed the stairs and exchanged her wedding finery for a comfortable sleeveless hip length pajama top and matching flowing pajama pants. She padded out of the room, went to each of the boys' rooms, tucked them in and kissed them goodnight.

They must be exhausted, or they wouldn't already be asleep!

The house was quiet as she walked down the hallway toward the stairs to be by her new husband in the drawing room downstairs.

Mark sat on the couch sipping a glass of wine looking like a picture of contentment as Alma entered the room. His right shoe clunked to the floor, making Alma smile. She curled up beside him, tucking her bare feet underneath her.

Hours ago, Mark had tossed his jacket over the back of the printed sofa, and his bow tie was all askew. He had rolled his shirt sleeves up several times, exposing his tanned, well-formed arms.

"You look comfortable. Why didn't you get changed?" she asked.

"No energy to climb the stairs. I'm so glad they've all left," Mark said. "I worried I would have to use force to get Fipper out of the house. The man is a lush! Preston should be getting back any minute. I sure hope he didn't deck the man—what a rotten mouth!"

"Why did he keep going on about bugs?" Alma asked.

"That was funny! He demanded to know why we never have bugs—you know, mosquitos, gnats, pesky flying things that are usually all over the place. Wouldn't shut up about it," Mark snickered.

"I told him I bought fifty gecko lizards and turned them loose on the yard so he'll probably put out inquiries all over town about them."

"Oh, Mark, you didn't!" she said, laughing uproariously. "Okay, now tell me how you got rid of the bugs."

"I zapped them!" he laughed. "Then I placed little invisible, silent zappers all over the place. Real simple."

"You're impossible, do you know that? You have to tolerate the good and bad in people. With Fipper, the bad part is the drinking; the good is that he's going to boost the economy of the exotic pet trade, or whoever handles geckos. At least it was a beautiful ceremony; our rings are gorgeous, Mark," she said gazing down at her soft, manicured hand.

He nuzzled her neck with tiny kisses and love bites. He bent away from her and set the glass down on the side table and took her in his arms.

"You haven't had the time to look, and I didn't have the time to show you—read the inscription on the inside of your ring," he said.

Curious about the mystique that Mark was creating, Alma slipped the beautiful wide band off her left hand. She turned it on its side, and read the strange message:

"To Xidiea, my only love. Hemlon"

She looked confused. She turned to Mark with a questioning look. "Xidiea and Hemlon? Are these antique rings that belonged to someone in your family?"

"No. Alma and Mark are Earth names and do not exist on Kredo; they will exist only while we are here. You were named Xidiea, and the name I am known by is Hemlon. Can you get used to that?" he asked.

"It will take time to get used to the strange names, but I don't dislike either of them. I'd like to go to Kredo soon. I want to know the place I was born; the place that seems so foreign to me. Even our real names are a challenge for me.

"I want to see my father and feel my mother's presence, which I know must be near him. There are so many things to do, and I don't want to prolong the journey," she said, burrowing into his arms.

"Let's go upstairs," he whispered, caressing her back as he pressed his lips onto hers. "I need you, Alma."

The cream-colored spread that had been tossed onto the floor looked like a shimmering sea bathed in moonlight.

Physical lovemaking intensified tenfold by the powerful mental illusions each of the lovers projected which ended the love session in total exhaustion.

Two entwined bodies lay soundly sleeping in the still of the night. The walls could fill volumes about the passion that ran rampant within their boundaries.

Sometime in the night, Mark woke and gently disengaged the sheet and covered Alma, then scooted under the protective warmth himself, falling back into the depths of sleep, content.

Morning poured brightly through the lace-covered windows and doused the room in sunny splendor, waking the sleeping tenants one by one. Mark opened his eyes to the sight of Alma curled into a ball, clutching the satin spread.

As the sunlight played on her eyes, they fluttered open. Alma lay in the sleep-awake state for a few minutes before stretching her limbs and turning to her other side to see Mark lying awake beside her.

"Good morning," he said, reaching out to her warm body, rubbing his hand along the curve of her hip. "Did you sleep well?"

"Uh huh. If I weren't starving, I'd lay here all morning, but it feels like I haven't eaten in days!" she said. "Are you hungry?"

"Starving," he said, raking his eyes across her luscious curves, his hands tracing a pattern on her willing flesh.

She slid her hand up his arm and caressed the sinewy limb. Mark leaned over her sprawled form on the creamy sheets. His mouth descended to her white breasts, teasing one, then the other with his tongue and hot lips.

Breakfast was forgotten as the two lovers satisfied a more important hunger. When they finally rose from the great bed, Alma glimpsed the clock.

"Eleven o'clock! I can't believe it's this late. We'd better get moving before someone comes looking for us," she said, disengaging herself from her husband's captive arms, and walking toward the bathroom. Twenty minutes later she joined Mark, fully dressed in black leggings and a hip-length loose top downstairs in the kitchen.

Cook bustled about in her hectic way, preparing meals for the rest of the day. Mark sat at the table drinking a cup of coffee when Alma entered.

He rose from his chair and came around to her side, kissing her as if he hadn't seen her in days, instead of minutes. He pulled her chair out for her and sat her at the large table, sitting across from her.

"Good morning, Cook," Alma said, affectionately.

"Morning, Missy," Cook replied, bringing a fresh cup of coffee and a plate of buttery biscuits and setting them in front of Alma. "My, wasn't that a lovely wedding? You looked like a fairy princess in that dress. All that was missing was a pair of wings and a magic wand!"

Cook stood with her hands clutched to her chest as she gazed into nothingness, dreamy-eyed. Alma held back a giggle and realized in that moment that romantic notions were not limited to starry-eyed Earth females. Cook was hooked on the white knight theory.

"Cook, you're an impossible romantic!" Alma said, blushing at the compliment. "Have you seen the boys?"

"I imagine they're about, getting into trouble, or at least planning on making trouble," she said.

At that minute, Preston entered the kitchen from the side door and greeted Mark and Alma. "Have you seen the boys, Preston?" Mark asked.

"They're probably with Spencer. I haven't seen them since breakfast," he said.

As if cued, Spencer came around the corner from the hallway, dressed with precise propriety down to his highly polished black shoes.

"Ah! Good morning Sir, Madame," the elder man said.

"Good morning Spencer. We were wondering if you had seen Cody and Jamie this morning," Alma asked.

"Now that you mention it, not since early this morning," he said.

A worried frown crossed Alma's face. "Where do you think they could have snuck off to?" she asked Mark. Turning to Preston, she asked when he last saw them.

"Around eight-thirty or nine o'clock I'm sure," he said. Preston was clearly worried.

"Perhaps they're out in the woods exploring," Mark said. "They should be coming in soon, Alma. They're going to get hungry and head straight for the kitchen."

"You're right, I just worry about them," she said. "They've never missed a meal yet, and knowing them, they took something with them."

"That they did," Cook said, a twinkle in her eyes. "I sent them off with some biscuits to get them out of the kitchen. I knew they weren't too interested in cleaning up after the wedding."

"Well at least they won't starve. I'm willing to bet that they'll be back by no later than one o'clock, Alma," Mark said, trying to reassure his wife.

Mark reached out and *sensed* the boys. They were goofing off and not getting into trouble.

"I just sensed them. They're in the woods," Mark said.

You two need to check in periodically Alma sent through mind-talk.

Okay Cody sent.

"I just told them to check in," Alma said.

"Come to think of it, the other day they were sneaking around the garage," Preston said. "I'll bet they found some of their old things and are out in the woods improvising some kind of clubhouse."

"Ah ha!" Mark exclaimed. "That's it in a nutshell. We'll give them some time, then hunt them down to see if they're staying out of trouble."

"I sensed them, but I didn't see where exactly in the woods they were."

"Cody said he would check in," Alma said.

"I don't mind their having a "secret" place; I just want to know where it is and if it's safe," Mark said.

Alma set her worries aside, finished her coffee and ate two of the scrumptious biscuits before leaving the comfort of the kitchen and wandering into the library.

She retrieved one of the Kredon history volumes from the table where she had left it and curled up on the couch to resume her lessons.

Jamie and Cody gloated over their stash of goods deep in the woods, inside the abandoned gardeners shed that now looked like a lean-to. A week earlier, the two had discovered the shelter and had claimed it.

On a quest for discovery, they had found the furniture from their old house in the rooms over the garage. They helped themselves to an old lantern, two low beach chairs, and Cody's old bedspread, for the floor.

Pleased that they had set up housekeeping without being detected, they had laughed and played for hours in the dilapidated "fort".

Their time was spent practicing the Kredon mind games that Preston and Spencer had taught them. There was a lot of practice ahead of them to become proficient at visualizing things, and they practiced every day.

Jamie and Cody learned that if they both closed their eyes and concentrated on the same thing, they could project an image of their concentration in front of them. The image was weak and would only last for two or three seconds after they opened their eyes.

Unable to tune into Kredo at this point, they had a favorite game where they encased themselves in their protective bubbles and tried to break through each other's barriers with either rocks or sticks.

They also tried mental attacks, which failed. The new powers intrigued the young boys, and they learned quickly.

Today they were in luck. With everyone busy cleaning away the wedding finery from yesterday, they could sneak away after breakfast with some of Cook's biscuits.

Cody did not avoid work if something needed to be done, but today he and Jamie wanted to try to get to Kredo through visualization.

The shed blended into the surrounding scenery. An observer would think it was an overgrown, dense area and would probably walk around the tangles and briars. The boys had found it by accident while chasing each other wildly through the woods playing tag.

Jamie had fallen down in front of the vine-covered open door with the old hinges rusted and frozen in position. Cody toppled over him and they both had stared at the perfect retreat with ideas zooming through their minds.

Intrigued with the setup, they had ventured inside, defying any spiders that may have nested in the cobwebbed entrance.

They didn't think an animal could have adopted the place for its home and were startled as a large rat rushed past them. It bumped into Cody as it ran out the doorway.

They both ran screaming out of the place as fast as their legs could carry them, stopping about fifty feet away.

After catching their breath, they decided to take another chance and go back inside and investigate.

Cody and Jamie armed themselves with sturdy branches and crept back inside the shed and adopted it as their own secret place.

They sat comfortably on the old bedspread and they laid plans and practiced. Not sure how their mentors did it, the boys tried locking their minds together as Preston and Spencer had done.

"Okay, let's try to think our brains together," Cody explained. "Do you remember the picture of the brain?"

Nodding, Jamie looked wide-eyed at his brother waiting for instructions.

"Think your brain inside my brain, or something like that," Cody said, using his hands coming together as an example

"Gotcha," Jamie said.

They sat silently and stared at each other, visualizing the feat.

"Wow! I could feel you right inside my head," Cody bellowed to his brother.

"I know! Wasn't that neat?" Jamie chirped.

After several experiments, they calmed down and got on with their task, locking their minds together.

"Let's go to that plant building!" Jamie said

They concentrated on the strange building on Kredo that had captured their senses and interest. At first only wavering flashes of some type appeared. They backed off and rested for a few minutes.

"Did you see that? We're making progress!" Cody said.

They tried to tune into the planet and exhausted their young minds. That was not enough of a barrier to stop them because they knew they could do the same things as Preston and Spencer.

Determination was high on their list of traits, and that alone would make them successful. Once again, they locked minds.

A faint mirage appeared before them, then disappeared. Both boys were overjoyed. They squealed with excitement and clapped their hands wildly.

"Do you want to try it again, Cody?" Jamie asked his older brother.

His eyes were wide with excitement.

"That was neat! Yeah, let's try it again. This time, lock your mind onto the building and don't let go. Ready?" Cody asked.

Jamie bobbed his head furiously.

They linked their minds together and conjured the scene before them. This time when they opened their eyes, they held fast to the image.

Cody experimented with his mind and tried to get inside the building, wanting to see the different stages of plant life once again.

"Don't do that!" Jamie squealed. "Stay outside with me!"

"Oh, don't be such a poop-head," Cody said. It was kind of strange, he agreed, and after second thoughts, he felt protective of his little brother and hugged him.

After ten or fifteen minutes of imagery play with the building, their mirage wavered and vanished, and was replaced with another image.

"Did you tune into a movie?" Jamie asked.

"I thought that was yours," Cody said.

An image of a group of strange men appeared, dressed in gray baggy pantaloons, tight black leather boots. Their muscular chests were bared, except for a black leather h-type strap studded with triangular metal decorations.

The stranger's heads were topped with a black helmet that rounded down to the bridge of their nose in front and to the back of their necks in the rear. They held weapons in their hands that looked like guns.

The boys watched with interest; the thrill of adventure hooked Jamie. Cody sat spellbound. Then, sensing danger, Cody quickly drew his brother to him and placed a protective shield around them both.

"Be real quiet, Jamie. Those bad men are looking for US," Cody whispered, scared.

"Put your shield with mine like Dad taught us so they can't get to us." Within minutes, their hide-away was blasted apart.

Before the huddled youngsters stood the menacing group from the apparition. Knowing they were in danger, Cody held his brother close.

"Let down your shield!" the leader boomed. He held his hand out in front of him and the air wavered.

His fierce-looking face with a black mustache and deep battle scars terrified Jamie long before his voice had sounded.

"Never! You won't get near us. Go away!" Cody yelled, clearly frightened. "I'll call my father and he'll come and get you!"

"Mommy! Daddy!" Jamie screeched. His eyes mirrored his fright.

"No one can hear you." The leader sneered at the boys.

The six men spread out around the huddled boys in their protective bubble shield. Without a nod or a sound, the whole group and the bubble vanished, leaving behind an eerie silence.

Mark emerged from the hidden room and found Alma curled up on the couch, engrossed in the Kredon history book.

"It's one-ten, Alma. Do you know if the boys have returned yet?" he asked.

Alma jumped and reprimanded Mark. "You scared me half to death! I don't think they've showed up yet because I haven't seen or heard them," she said. "Let me call out to them."

Cody! Jamie! You need to come home.

Alma glanced at the clock.

Mark checked his watch. *Cody! You and your brother get home now or you're in big trouble.*

"I'm pretty sure that will light a fire under them," Alma said.

She and Mark chuckled.

Still, there was no response from the boys.

"Something's not right. I'm sure they wouldn't stay away this long. They usually stick pretty close to Preston and Spencer," Mark said, brooding over the facts.

He reached out his senses, but did not detect either of his sons.

"Something's happened to them, hasn't it?" Alma said, fear sounding in her voice as she quickly got up and walked toward the kitchen with Mark.

"I don't sense them now," he said.

First, they checked with Cook, then summoned Spencer and Preston. The boys hadn't returned.

"Let's check out the woods," he said to Preston.

"Alma, you, Spencer and Cook search the house. Open your senses fully."

The five worried people split up, each calling the boys names verbally and silently as they searched.

Every closet and corner in the large house was checked, including the secret room and the silent, empty attic.

Spencer rushed over to the garage and searched the garage and the rooms overhead. It was clear that the boys had been there.

Crumbs were on the otherwise clean floor, and small fingerprints showed in the dust on surfaces. There was no sign of either boy hiding there now.

Mark and Preston tramped through the woods calling out the boys' names; they used their minds to scan the dense area.

There were miles of beautiful homes nestled among the towering trees. The expensive home-sites prided themselves on their natural setting keeping the lovely giants that other developers cut down.

Now, though, it was a problem. The neighboring estates were all large and densely wooded, making the search difficult.

Mark stopped briefly and called out silently for Preston to join him. In minutes, Preston emerged and hurried to Mark's side.

"We need to do this logically if we're ever going to accomplish anything," Mark said, projecting a sectioned map in the air in front of them. "Here's where I've covered. Where have you been?"

Similar to a computerized map, the different sections lit up in fluorescent colors denoting where each had searched. As they parted, they agreed to keep updating the map so they could monitor their progress.

They continued the search; each kept a vision of the map, and as they walked through the woods, their paths were outlined luminously. Minutes ticked past.

After twenty minutes, Mark projected an image of himself to Preston.

"I'm changing sectors; there's nothing in the area where I've been checking. Here's where I will try. There are a few old buildings that they've probably staked out," he said.

"Okay. I think I'll try over here where we found that old tire swing hanging from that huge oak tree," Preston said, pointing to the area.

They each separated once more.

As the men walked, the lines on the map continued to move forward. Preston approached the swing and probed the area.

No new vibrations.

Friday's visit was apparent, but the boys hadn't played there since. Preston studied the map to see where he could continue his hunt and was deciding between the Smithey's property or the Pemberton's.

Thinking that the Smithey's duck pond might be conducive to a boyish attack, he went there.

As Preston glanced over to Mark's quadrant, he was shocked as the illuminated line suddenly disappeared.

Inside the house, the three searchers joined each other in the garden room, a sunny room with huge glass panels that opened onto a lovely terrace. The wooden floor, covered with a huge, colorful wool rug, butted against a tiled, raised floor filled with tropical plants of every kind.

Nerves frayed, Alma sank onto the padded lounge chair, one of several pieces of furniture graced by the lovely rug.

Worried, Cook wrung her hands on the dishtowel she carried, and Spencer gazed out the plant-filled windows toward the heavily wooded area surrounding the house.

"Don't worry, Missy. They're probably out playing and forgot what time it is. I'm sure their stomachs are calling for them to come in for a food raid right about now," Cook said, trying to ease tension.

"They've never done this before! Cody is a responsible little boy and wouldn't intentionally stay away," Alma said. "Where in the world do you think they went?"

"No telling, Miss Alma," Spencer added. "This house is surrounded by at least twelve acres of woods and three other estates; parts of it are pretty dense. Don't you worry. Master Mark will find the tots and bring them back. There's squirrels, rabbits, and even a few deer out there, plus plenty of wooden fences to climb over—so much for young boys to explore."

"I'll ground them for a week when they get back! Darn those two, they are old enough for a little common sense," Alma declared.

"Now, now. Don't be too hard on them, Missy. Remember your old house? This place is a boy's dream. Brings out the adventurer in them," Cook said.

The three stood and paced and waited a hellish long time, growing restless as the minutes passed with imaginations running amok.

An electrified tension filled the air causing the fine hairs to stand erect on Alma's arms. With no other warning, a transparent evil vision appeared before them, sending fingers of fear clutching their hearts.

Asedi!

"Surrender your claim to rule Kredo, or your children shall die," boomed the voice from the gray-hooded, withered man.

Alma sprang off the lounge chair and shrouded the vision with a mind probe.

A mocking, maniacal laugh filled the room and chilled her.

"That doesn't work, my dear. You have so much to learn. Tsk tsk, too bad," the evil voice laughed. The vision wavered and vanished leaving the room heavy with emotion.

Running footsteps grew louder bringing Preston into the room. He panted for breath and stopped before the three shocked people.

Chest heaving, he talked in gasps.

"An old shed out in the woods. Gone!" he gasped. "Taken by force."

Alma rushed to Preston's side, placed one hand on his arm, the other on his back. "We know, Preston. Asedi was here; he's taken the boys. Where's Mark?"

"Gone! One minute he was there, the next minute he vanished. I didn't feel his presence anywhere!" the anguished man said.

Chapter 12

An eruption of fear and anger swelled inside Alma, clutching her heart, making her breath raspy.

She forced calming feelings through the catalyst of emotions raging through her and brought her pounding heart under control.

Now, of all times, she must remain calm, in complete command of her emotions. Much was at stake: the safety of her sons and the whereabouts of her husband.

She closed her eyes and reached deep inside her mind for the resources stored there, given to her by her husband not long ago. She sought answers, power, strength.

Energy burst forth from somewhere deep within her mind, focusing on the closed room, turning the peaceful retreat into a tumultuous air pocket.

Her shirt rippled about her body, snapping in the hectic winds that swirled about her.

The hanging plants swayed crazily from their hooks. The floor plants toppled over and leaves broke off and flew about the room in mini whirlwinds.

She reached toward the heavens, hair flaring wildly in the storm, and she called out to her husband then to her children in a strange language.

Silence answered, confirming her worst fears.

If they had been anywhere on Earth, she would have had a response from one of them.

Alma dug deeper inside and sought other methods of reaching out. A void greeted her. Devastation hit her as she realized she had truly lost contact with her family.

With sorrow overwhelming all of her reasoning functions, she calmed the storm inside the room, returning the stillness that had been prevalent.

The quiet room looked a mess with potting soil and broken foliage strewn about. A lamp had fallen from its perch atop a table and lay in a pool of broken glass from the shattered light bulb. A number of pages from a magazine fluttered down toward the floor.

Her shoulders drooped in defeat, letting her head bend down wearily.

"You cannot give up so easily! Many hurdles lie ahead in your path and you are the only one who can overcome them. Believe me when I say there are powers deep within you that do not compare to any others," Cook said sternly.

The older woman determined that her mistress needed a push in the right direction, otherwise pity would stake its claim, crippling her forever. This was the woman that would one day rule Kredo, her beloved world. She would not let anything hold the mistress back this early in the game.

Alma heard the strength in those words and sank down to a clear spot on the floor. She crossed her legs and rested her head in her hands. Eyes closed, elbows supported on her knees, she journeyed to the depths of the past neatly tucked away in her head. The knowledge waited for her to claim and use it. She needed to understand her genetic makeup, her power and to understand how to use it.

She bet her parents never contemplated how Earth life would affect their only child. Their plans never took into consideration how difficult it would be for her to discover her true self and pull it all together.

Alma realized she needed guidance. The staid life she had led with "Aunt Rose" and "Uncle Donald" had been entirely devoid of true responsibility, and her former marriage had been little better.

As she sat in stony silence, the servants eased quietly out of the room, knowing that their mistress was probing deep within herself for a solution. They all more or less deduced the same thing.

It had been a mistake to withhold her heritage and all that knowledge. Now that she needed those resources, she couldn't find them, or if she did, they wondered, would she understand what to do with them?

Alma reached into a depth of her subconscious that had been buried deeper than other bits of knowledge for reasons unknown to her. She found what she needed and immediately unfolded herself to the lesson before her.

Yes. That is exactly what I seek. Why didn't I think of this before?

Through manipulation of body chemicals and molecules due to her Kredon heritage, she stepped outside of herself and momentarily glanced down at her physical body sitting quietly on the floor. She nodded her approval and padded quietly on bare feet toward the kitchen where the others waited patiently.

As she passed a mirror, she stopped to glance at the bizarre image it presented to her. She gazed at herself in wonderment. She appeared sparkling, ethereal—not entirely solid.

This was entirely different from the lesson Mark had taught her. She projected herself in a way where she would not be seen by anyone from Earth, but she would be visible to Kredons.

Alma continued to the kitchen. When she arrived, the three inhabitants immediately stopped talking to stare at the vision before them.

"You've done well," Preston said quietly.

Spencer studied Alma. "When you travel through space your body will not be a dense mass. Only when you are on solid ground will your body resume its corporeal form, so great caution is called for. Use your senses to protect yourself.

"Make no mistake about the dangers that surround you while you search, Miss Alma. These two bodies are bound to each other. If you are injured while away from your solid body here on Earth, you must find a way to heal yourself. Your earth body can perish as well as your traveling body."

"Go now, before the trail becomes cold. We will come when summoned," Cook said.

Nodding, Alma closed her eyes tightly, bent her head back so she faced the ceiling and immediately vanished.

Preston, Spencer and Cook quickly walked to the garden room and stood in specific locations around their mistress' physical body.

They silently stared at an invisible central spot causing an undetectable shield to envelope her vulnerable form, secreting her from prying eyes.

If anyone approached, they would see an empty room. If anyone other than the three servants walked through the room, they would be redirected automatically from the spot where she sat.

Only Kredons would be able to detect their mistress. There was so much at stake. Asedi could send a force of power to thwart Alma's mission. Preston, Spencer and Cook had to do what they could to prevent anything hazardous from happening.

They focused their power once again; the disastrous room became the peaceful setting of an hour ago without a leaf out of place. As the three left the room, Cook stopped, turning to face her mistress, then scanned the room once more for danger. Satisfied that everything was in order, she hurried to catch up with her companions.

Black, cold and infinite time whizzed past, along with a deafening roar from the speed which accompanied the unique space travel.

The absence of a vehicle didn't matter. Not being solid, objects passed through and around her. Although she didn't have to worry about the effects of the journey on her physical body, Alma did have to worry about other factors.

She would become a solid form on Kredo rather than the misplaced molecular mass she had appeared to be on Earth in the projected form. She would have to worry about her physical body there, the risks were great.

If anything happened to her while she was on Kredo, it would affect her Earth body in some way. She would have to be wary of everything; otherwise she might possibly never be whole again.

Alma pondered that horror, putting it foremost in her mind. She was glad Spencer had spelled out the urgency of her situation.

As she sped through the universe past galaxies, Alma was amazed at what she experienced.

At first, she had rushed her hands before her face fearing she would crash into something solid. But when she understood how the projection worked, she watched everything whiz past her and through her, amazed.

Dead planets, places just beginning to develop, and worlds teeming with bizarre life forms held her spellbound.

Brilliant suns splashing their fire out around them, and dark, dead moons were wondrous to see.

Alma approached Ecko, the prison moon. Craggy mountains and a dull brown surface devoid of vegetation was all she saw. No water was visible and not even one cloud roamed the skyline.

There were no buildings. She wondered where the prison was. As she floated over the surface she spied a huge door of an unknown material built into one of the mountains.

Suddenly she staggered. Alma realized she was on solid ground once again; she had arrived at her destination.

But, where was she?

She tried to sense her whereabouts. Alma figured this was one of the lower levels of the underground prison structure, but not quite at the dungeons.

Alma got her bearings and looked around and began putting her notions into motions. She moved stealthily down the narrow, sloping, ill-lit corridor, she took in her surroundings while listening intently to every sound.

The granite-type walls and slab floors were layered with dust and spider webs. A pathway down the center of the corridor showed faint footprints in the scattered dust.

Alma guessed that guards made periodic rounds, but not very often. Cobwebs were profuse toward the ceiling masking the inset, insufficient lights, and throwing menacing shadows on walls and floors.

A long stretch of corridor barren of doors was before her. Halfway to the end she discovered another dimly lit corridor, this one having several recessed doors.

Cautiously, she crept down the dusty corridor, keeping close to the wall, stopping periodically to listen for any noise. A faint stench of excrement and rotting flesh assailed her.

What horror lies ahead? She shuddered. She thought of the lunatic in charge and assumed Asedi probably had a well-used dungeon or two hidden away. That was most likely what she smelled—rotting flesh. The waft of a forgotten body made her stomach queasy, but she forced herself to go on.

She came upon the first door and listened for any sound from within, then set her fine-tuned senses to work to see if the cell contained any life.

Convinced there wasn't an occupant, she stood on her tip-toes and peeked through the short bars. Dust-laden, black chains rested against the wall, waiting to be filled once again. The tiny cell was empty. The next three cells proved to be the same.

As Alma continued, the odor grew more offensive, making her stomach lurch several times. She fought to control the powerful nausea. Surely there was a way for her to block the stench? She wouldn't be able to take the time to explore that skill now.

All the other cells appeared empty and looked as if they hadn't been used in a decade. The corridor curved to the east and appeared less traveled with thicker dust, and the ceilings heavier with cobwebs which provided less light than the one she just left.

Practically gagging from the foul air, Alma covered her nose and mouth with the short sleeve of the shirt. She forced herself to breathe through her mouth, keeping her nose blocked for as long as possible.

The next cell housed a skeleton that told a gruesome story. Stretched out full length, shackled at the ankle, with fingers bent from clawing the floor, the unfortunate man must have tried to reach the food and water bowls. Someone had cruelly placed them inches out of his reach.

What type of person would do such a thing?

Overcome with emotion as she finally turned from the door, Alma had horrible opinions about the jailers running through her mind. To let a human being die in such a way was inexcusable! She vowed that this would never happen under her watch!

The skeleton wasn't the cause of the defiling odor. Those bones hadn't seen flesh in at least fifty years, she assumed. Alma peeked into four more cells, all empty.

The fifth proved interesting. Ajar barely a quarter of an inch, the fifth cell door drew her like a magnet. She used extreme caution and raised onto her tip-toes and peeked into the darkened cell. It appeared to be empty.

With nerves leashed, she tugged the door open. The old hinges respected her prayers of silence.

The tiny cubicle looked barren of any past inhabitants. In one dark corner, however, there appeared to be a crude opening, perhaps a burrow of a large rodent.

As Alma approached the hole, she studied it. She thought it was manmade. She stooped down in front of the opening on all fours, she peered inside the pitch-black hole.

She wished she had a light with her. She looked around the room and abandoned the thought. There was nothing here to help her.

The more she studied it the more she thought there was something compelling about this tunnel.

Where did it lead?

Something told her a human had dug it, and perhaps there was an ally inside these dismal walls. Standing once again, she turned and walked toward the door.

She listened before opening the door to pass through and detected the sound of footsteps approaching in the distance. Instinctively, she hastily pushed the door so it would appear closed as it had been when she came upon it.

The heavy marching footsteps rounded the corner and headed her way.

Alma ran to the opposite side of the tiny cell and dove into the tunnel and hurried forward until she was sure she was out of sight.

She could barely squeeze to one side of the tunnel wall and look over her shoulder to see if she had been detected.

A moment of panic assailed her. She hastily shot her hand out in the direction from where she came and wiggled her fingers. Her footprints were erased.

Alma didn't know where that knowledge came from, but she happily applied the newfound tool. When she peeked through the tunnel opening, undisturbed dust covered the cell floor.

She scooted away from the tunnel opening. All was still around her except for the pounding of her heart in a wild tempo. The sound of rushing blood and her hammering heart filled her ears to a deafening crescendo. As she forced her body under control, she strained for the sounds of danger.

The heavy footsteps were close by. As Alma huddled on all fours, crouched as close to the floor as possible without laying down, she listened as the intruder marched past. She probed the guard's mind to determine what to do next.

"Two more levels to go. I don't know why we bother to check down here, anyway. All this dust. Who's going to break out of a cell and hide down here?" the guard mumbled.

Alma breathed a silent sigh of relief, making her heart feel lighter than it had only minutes before. She used instinct as a guide and crept slowly forward, being careful of how much pressure she placed on her knees.

The leggings were made from thin material for the Houston summer.

Alma continued to crawl forward. She wondered if it was her imagination or perhaps her adjustment to the darkness, but she thought she could detect the tunnel around her.

She assumed light was filtering through from somewhere. The anticipation excited and frightened her, not having any way of knowing what lay ahead of her.

She prayed that this was a manmade tunnel, not some large creature's roadway leading directly to its home. She would have to face unknown possibilities when she came upon either a den or freedom.

The footsteps had faded in the distance and the foul odor had all but disappeared as Alma crept forward. She determined that she had been steadily going deeper into the prison and this tunnel would eventually lead to the dungeons hidden deep below the surface of Ecko.

She felt as if she had been crawling for miles and had no way of judging the distance, except for her bruised extremities. For a long stretch, the roof was high enough for her to sit up and rest her knees, which sadly needed a break.

Alma sat in the dark with her back against one wall with her feet against the other wall; she let her mind wander.

She didn't detect the boys or Mark's presence anywhere, but she realized they might be inside these old walls, in someone else's mind bubble.

She wondered about her physical body on Earth.

Was it feeling anything she was experiencing? She seemed real where she was now; complete. She even looked complete.

It would take time for her to understand these new skills and to sort out everything.

She ended her break and unfolded her body and continued on. After approximately a fifty-foot stretch, the tunnel became shallow, and she was forced to stretch out on her belly and pull herself forward with her hands.

Alma was thankful the floor was smooth and free of rocks or debris. She continued, aware that her hands were taking a beating. She tried to use her palms and finger pads without digging her fingernails into the solid surface.

At this point, she couldn't care less about her manicure. She was more worried about being able to use her hands when she needed them at the end of this tunnel.

As she pulled forward the tunnel curved, and at one point she had a difficult time getting around the curvature. She had to use her feet along the wall to propel herself forward.

When she finally made the turn, she was delighted to see an end to the dark void.

Light! Faint, but up ahead a bit, a light shone through like a beacon in a dark sky.

It seemed like hours before she finally crawled to the end of the darkness. Being ever so cautious, she inched closer to the opening. When she was to the point of being barely hidden by darkness, she stayed still and looked about, taking in her new surroundings.

Alma probed with her senses. She detected no danger. She had come upon another tiny cell, similar to the ones that she had left behind.

Silence greeted her as she looked around as much as the confining tunnel would allow. Satisfied that the cell was unoccupied, she crept forward, anxious to leave the restricting tunnel.

A slight scuffling sound in a corner of the cell, out of her range of vision, stopped her dead in her tracks. If something happened to enter the tunnel, she would not be able to retreat. She would have to face it head on.

Her heart pounded as she waited for something to happen. She dared not retreat to the welcoming darkness for fear of making a sound that would alert whoever, or whatever moved in the room.

She feared being attacked by an animal.

Without warning, the head and upper torso of a human body darted into the tunnel blocking her light. Each of them gasped loudly with fright, and suddenly, a dirty, withered hand darted out and clamped over her mouth.

Alma let out a squeak of fear.

Don't make a sound! the Kredon voice said in her mind. *Can you be quiet?*

Eyes wide with fright, Alma nodded, and the hand drew back.

Come, he said inside her head as he backed out of the tunnel, holding a finger to his lips.

Alma hesitated a minute. She then crept forward, crawling out into the tiny room. Before her squatted an old man, age undiscernible.

He wore tattered pantaloons and what was left of a tunic; his parchment feet were bare. Gray hair and beard, matted and dirty, had long ago been left unattended.

He scooted back as she came fully into the room.

She figured he was either giving her room to get up or keeping a safe distance until he knew he was safe—she was an intruder.

Not wanting to show aggression, Alma slowly stood up. Her back and legs silently screamed their agony, causing her to wince in pain. She rubbed her knees, then her back, before rubbing her hands together; she was covered with scrapes and nicks.

The old man eyed her suspiciously, then, he stood. She sensed that his old body was not used to being upright. His back hunched over and it was impossible to determine what his height might have been at one time.

I did not mean to alarm you, she said inside his mind. *Asedi kidnapped my sons and I am searching for them. I am Xidiea. Can you help me?* she pleaded.

Wonderment crossed the old man's face. *Xidiea, daughter of Reena and Jetron?* he asked with familiarity.

Yes. You know of my parents? she asked, surprised.

Yes! Yes! he said, tears misting his eyes. *I was your father's manservant for many, many years before the revolution. The old Keeper had me brought here long ago and put someone else in my place at Cralic Sector. You were just a tiny babe then.*

What is your name, old man? Alma asked.

Bejion. Is that name in your mind someplace? he asked.

She closed her eyes tight and pressed her fingers to her temples. *Yes! You are in my memories! My God, how long have you been here, Bejion?*

Many, many years. I do not know how long. What is your age? You were still in the cradle when I last gazed upon your infant face, he said, his mind wandering into his memories.

Alma shook her head in disbelief. *Bejion, I am twenty-eight years old. You have been here all this time? How have you survived?*

The old man blinked several times. *They don't know I'm here. Figured I died, they did.*

Did you dig the tunnel? Alma asked.

Just two. Dozens of tunnels around here. Go all over the place. They think they're gromi burrows, Bejion said.

Noticing her confusion, he asked her if she knew what a gromi was. She told him no.

They're about this big, he said, holding his hands to show the size.

Alma tried to get a picture of the animal in her mind but decided they must be about the size of a border collie in both length and height.

Ornery things, too. Look like someone stepped on their face, all pushed in and wrinkly; short little ears and gray skin. No tail. Love to burrow. Haven't seen one in a long time; guess they moved on, not enough bugs for them to eat here. Where have you been? he asked, completely changing the subject.

I've spent all my life on a planet called Earth, with two of my parents most trusted servants. I really don't know that much about Kredo or Ecko, but I'm learning as I go along. Hemlon has taught me a lot. Did you know him? she asked.

Yes, yes, I did. Good little boy. Your parents arranged for you to marry him. Must be all grown up by now. Did you do it—marry him? Bejion asked.

Yes, we just got married yesterday. Tears misted her eyes. Knowing she couldn't let go of her stored emotions, Alma squelched the tears that threatened to burst and took control once more.

Bejion, what do you eat? How do you live here?

I've got a tunnel to the food larder. Just go and help myself when no one's around, he said, smiling.

Well, why in the world haven't you left Ecko? Alma asked.

How am I going to do that? No one knows I'm alive. Everyone believed I died when they were going to put that little thing in my head. Tricked them, I did. Stopped my heart. They threw my body on the heap, he said, a sad look on his face.

Is that what I smelled back there? she asked, nodding in the direction of the tunnel.

Yup, sure is. They just throw the dead bodies onto a heap and spray a chemical on them so they'll decompose faster. Then they just dump the dust and bones someplace, he explained. *I got out of there real quick before they sprayed that stuff on me. Sure didn't want to get eaten up with chemicals after all that!*

A vivid picture crossed Alma's mind, causing her stomach to lurch, sending a rush of bile up to her throat. After several seconds, she conquered the weakness and settled down.

If you didn't have the disc implanted in your head, why didn't you call for help? Jetron would have come for you!

With a blank expression, Bejion looked at Alma and blinked. *Couldn't project that far. Don't have friends here, just been waiting. You're here now. You can rescue me,* he said, convinced that the problem was solved.

Deeply saddened, Alma closed her eyes momentarily. This man had lost all those years. Now, all he had was this bent, old body, his wasted mind that hardly functioned properly, and a way of life that couldn't be duplicated anywhere else.

Yes, I've rescued you. I'm so glad that I found you! As soon as I'm finished here, we're going home, she said, hugging him and swaying.

Tears welled up in her dark green eyes as judgements of all the repercussions of the revolution came flooding forth. The dam broke, releasing racking sobs from deep within her

Patting her arm with his bony hand, Bejion comforted Alma. "Don't cry. Don't cry. I'm your friend," he said, his voice crackly from lack of use.

Chapter 13

*G*oing home? Bejion asked, stupefied, after Alma's tears had dried. He looked around.

What's she talking about? I'm home.

His addled brain was lost in the fuzzy recess that hid his other life.

Yes, home—to Kredo, where you used to live, Alma explained. *Cralic Sector. You remember, my father's palace?*

Jetron's palace? Bejion asked.

Yes, she said. *Did you have friends there?* She tried to get his focus back on his former life.

Friends?

Alma sighed in exasperation and decided to let the subject drop. Bejion had lost almost all of his past from the years of harsh survival on Ecko and was too confused to understand anything.

He squatted on his haunches. The little man sat quietly, staring into space. A scene flashed through his mind, causing his brow to crease. A tall, stately brown-haired man in a long robe, standing in a white room; *He knew that man, didn't he?*

Bejion, have any new prisoners arrived today? Young prisoners, my sons? Alma asked, interrupting his trip to the past. She gave him a few minutes to anchor his mind then projected a picture of the boys to him, hoping the question would sink into the old man's intelligence.

No. None today. Many days go by sometimes before anyone new comes. They come and they go, he prattled in a singsong voice like a nursery rhyme.

A scene of a witnessed torture roared through his brain, causing him to squeeze his eyes shut tight. He clutched his head with his calloused hands and whimpered with the memory flooding his mind.

Alma stole a peek inside his head and was shocked at the depravity she witnessed. She covered her mouth with her hand and shuddered at what else this man had seen. As the minute passed, a semblance of normalcy returned. Blinking, Bejion looked at Alma and she realized that he expected her to continue with the previous conversation.

I don't sense them here either, she said, settling down to sit on the dirt floor, allowing her mind to wander. *I was sure Asedi would bring them here.*

It's not safe for us to stay here; the guards may come by. Come with me, let's sit in peace and quiet so you can talk out loud, Bejion said in a minute of rationality while tugging Alma to her feet. Alma stood and quirked an eyebrow at his choice of words.

What could be quieter? This place is like a crypt.

Bejion crossed to the opposite side of the tiny cell and grabbed the heavy, black chain on the wall attached to a shackle. While pulling the chain, he walked backwards and to the left.

A great block of the wall swung silently open exposing a dark tunnel. On the inside of the block hung another shorter chain with a large, black metal ring, which he used to pull the block back in place.

Hours of work had been put into smoothing the granite block in strategic places so it would slide quietly back and forth.

Go inside. I will close the door, he said, instructing her as if she were a child.

Alma rubbed her knees once more and began the grueling task of crawling on her hands and knees. She left more than enough room for Bejion; she stopped and waited for him to close off the tunnel and give her directions.

She barely heard the block slide into place; darkness surrounded her once more, reminding her of the task ahead.

Go ahead about fifteen feet. The tunnel widens at that point and I will pass you to lead the way, he explained, in control of his mind once again. *There are many tunnels off this one and you don't want to make a wrong turn.*

Alma crawled forward slowly, counting the paces. At approximately the correct distance, Bejion scooted past her.

He must have eyes like a mole, and his knees must have huge calluses on them from the years of crawling through these tunnels.

She wouldn't last more than a few yards; her knees and toes were tender, and her hands were slowly turning into raw meat; there wasn't an easier way to crawl.

How in the world did babies crawl until they learned to walk upright? It had never occurred to her how tough they were until this test of endurance.

Bejion must have realized that she was tender so he slowed his pace.

We will turn left soon. You will have to sense for the opening because you are not familiar with the route.

Alma crawled with one shoulder against the wall as a guide and went as fast as her body allowed. Only a thin layer of cloth acted as a buffer between the wall and her sore flesh.

Within minutes, the solid surface fell away and she tottered on hand and knees without the wall for support. She stopped and reached out to the opposite wall to determine the size of the opening.

It was large; probably on purpose, to allow a body to make the turn around the sharp corner.

We are almost there, Bejion said inside her mind.

Alma barely perceived his scurrying up ahead of her.

Mice probably make more noise than him.

The tunnel curves to the right. Be careful that you don't crash into the wall, he warned.

She slowed her pace and awkwardly reached out in front of her with one hand while balancing with the other and scooting forward.

After several feet, she came in contact with a solid wall in front of her. She was grateful Bejion had warned her. If she hadn't known of its existence, she would have slammed into it, probably knocking herself out. She swiped her hand across the wall and discovered the curve to the right.

Instinct told her that Bejion had stopped somewhere ahead of her in the dark void. A scraping noise caused Alma to turn her head sharply to her right.

There was nothing but the velvet darkness.

She reached out to touch the opposite wall and couldn't find it. She groped forward with one hand out in front of her as she became disoriented.

The walls had vanished, abandoning her in total darkness. Fright and confusion mingled when she flayed her arms out around her and didn't contact any solid surface.

Alma knelt in an upright position and carefully lifted her arms over her head.

No roof. The low roof of the tunnel had deserted her to the darkness.

Thank God the floor remained solid.

She sat back on her legs and gathered her wits about her. A sound similar to coarse sandpaper scraping against wood attacked her hearing. She jerked her head toward the noise, then suddenly, bright light produced by an old, battered lantern blinded her.

Alma withdrew her outstretched arm to her side and blinked while her eyes adjusted to the light.

They were in a large cavernous room, not quite high enough to allow her to stand upright, but she was able to hunch over and stretch her limbs.

She now understood why Bejion had not stood up easily in the tiny cell. It was a luxury that was rarely afforded to him.

All the comforts of home.

She looked around the dismal room. In one corner was a stack of old, dirty, thin mattresses, and several tattered blankets, probably from the guards' quarters.

An old metal cup, dish and knife were the sole utensils and looked like they were from the gold rush days in California. The battered lantern was the only source of light available in the room, showing three other tunnel openings.

Alma doubted if any other person was aware of this place's existence. It was cool and dry with clean air to breathe.

"This is your home," she stated out loud, sadly, thinking of the life Bejion had come from. The man was a survivor; he was strong-willed to have survived this grueling life after an easy life in the palace.

How did he first get into this lifestyle?

His jailers must not have kept track of the number of tunnels, the missing items Bejion had stolen from them, or the food.

Alma wondered how he had stumbled upon this place, and where he had slept until he established this place as home.

She guessed he must have followed the rodents around and learned their various tunnels.

How long had it taken him to find food and water?

She sat on the hard floor and drew her knees up and wrapped her arms around her tender limbs; she rubbed the scraped flesh with her bruised hands. She couldn't determine which felt worse, her hands, knees, shoulders or toes.

"Where would Asedi hide someone, Bejion?" she asked, hoping his mind was still sharp.

"Far, far away. Not here. He has enemies here who are loyal to your father. Can't hide anyone here in the prison," he said, lapsing into a blank stare.

"Far away where? Do you know any of the places where Asedi hides?" she coaxed, sensing the futility of the situation.

Bejion's eyes went in and out of focus. It was impossible for his mind to hold onto a subject for long, and this was one of his "out" periods.

Alma rested her chin on her knees and let her mind wander across the surfaces of two planets and one moon probing, searching for signs, drifting words, or anything that seemed familiar to her—any type of clue.

She wondered if Mark was with the boys, then quickly rejected the idea. Asedi would keep them separate, fearing the great power force of the three together.

So many places to hide and no clues.

Alma's frustration peaked as she sat in silent contemplation. She closed her eyes, succumbing to the lethargy easing into her weary body. She leaned slowly to the side, so tired.

In her mind's eye, a vivid picture of Cody and Jamie physically jerked her out of the dream-state.

She sat ramrod straight and opened her eyes.

Alma stared at the wall in front of her, neither seeing it nor anything else around her but locking her mind onto the vision inside her head.

Bejion sensed the electricity coursing through his companion and peeked into her mind: A vision of two young blond-haired boys huddled together under a protective shield surrounded by guards.

The room could be anywhere in the galaxy.

Silently calling out to her sons, she waited for a response, looked for a sign that they heard her. Nothing.

Why was she seeing them?

She didn't understand the logic.

Were they projecting and not knowing they did?

She scanned the area carefully, looking for a clue that would show her where they were being held. Something on the far wall, in between two of the guards caught her eye. It looked like a crest of some type. A silver star outlined several times was inset in the polished wall.

One guard moved slightly, obstructing her view. Alma cursed at him and had the urge to violently thrust him out of the way.

Instead, she looked at the room, training her eyes to search for details.

The wall that held the crest looked like dark gray marble polished to a high shine.

Heavy wine-colored velvet draperies covered long, wide windows in the large room with the high ceiling.

Are they in the palace, for heaven's sake? Surely it isn't an obvious place, is it?

She was furious that she had so little information to go by and certain things she had to learn as time went on.

"Jamie. Cody," she whispered out loud.

"Mother!" Cody yelled with his mind. "Where are you? Can you see us?"

"Cody! Yes, I can see you. Do you know where you are?" Alma said, her voice rising with anxiety. "Has anyone said anything that would help me find you?"

"No, mother. We've been in this room since we got here. Are you coming to get us? We're hungry," the young boy said, frightened.

"Cody, I can't find you. This room might not be on Kredo. Don't let down your shield for one minute! Try to contact your father. I'm sure he is nearby. In the meantime, I'm going to try to find out where you are so I can come and get you and Jamie. Take care of your little brother. I love you both," she said.

The vision vanished and was replaced with a weak vision of Mark lying on a white raised surface in a supine position.

"Xidiea . . ." he moaned.

Fear clutched at her heart. There was an unknown danger surrounding her husband.

Behind the closed doors of the secret room, Preston and Spencer searched for Mark in a mysterious way.

With minds locked together forming a dome over a projected vision of the wooded area surrounding the back of the house, they probed the area.

After twenty minutes of intense searching, the two separated, releasing their minds and hands, then breathing deeply.

"If we only knew where he was taken after Asedi captured him," Preston said.

"We'll find him; don't worry. It will just take a little more time," Spencer told his friend. "I wonder how Miss Alma is making out."

"She'll do just fine," Preston said. "There's no stopping her now. She has the power."

"Yes, she has the power, but she doesn't understand how to use it yet, and that worries me," Spencer nagged.

"The knowledge is there, and it will come to her when she needs it. All she has to learn is how to summon it," Preston said, defending his mistress.

"We know that, but does Miss Alma? I just hope she doesn't get into any trouble," Spencer hissed back. He was consumed with worry.

"She won't! She can take care of herself," Preston said brusquely. "Let's go get a cup of coffee and see Cook before we add to the problems."

The two men left the room, securing it behind them. As they walked out of the library, Spencer turned, surveying the room to make sure that everything was in order. Satisfied, he closed the double doors and joined Preston.

With the boys missing, Cook was not her jolly self. There were no children to bake for, no little ones to care for. As her friends entered the room, she raised her head off her hands and gave the men a questioning glance.

Preston shook his head, sighed and sat down. Cook moped once again and rested her chin in the palms of her hands.

"The whole family is gone! My babies are in danger, and we can't find master Mark! Was it wise for Miss Alma to go off like that?" Cook wailed, questioning herself for giving her mistress the push.

"Now, now, Gwever! Calm yourself," Spencer said to the frayed cook. "Yes, you did the right thing. She can't be protected forever, you know."

Shocked at hearing her formal name, Cook snapped out of her mental pit and sat straight in the chair. "Oh my, we're falling apart at the seams, aren't we?"

"Why don't the three of us have a nice hot cup of coffee and settle down?" Preston suggested. "We've got to keep things under control and do our best at solving the puzzle of finding master Mark. We can't afford to waste our powers worrying and squabbling."

"Here! Sit down, sit down," Cook said, jumping up to bustle about the kitchen. She gathered cups and saucers and placed them on a black lacquered tray, then poured the steaming black coffee into the three cups.

Next, she placed the sugar bowl, creamer and three spoons onto the tray and brought it to the table. After serving the men, she placed her cup on the table and sat down.

Silent fears flew through their minds as the three friends sat quietly drinking coffee. The stillness was needed so each of them could work out their worries and not disrupt the perfect balance of harmony among them. Minutes passed and cups drained. Turning to Spencer, Preston nodded.

"Let's go, shall we?" Spencer said to his friend. "This time we won't fail!" Preston, Spencer and Cook rose from the table.

Preoccupied with ideas bouncing in her head, Cook gathered up the dishes, keeping busy while the two men left the kitchen and returned to the secret room once again.

Preston and Spencer stood facing each other in the secret room and projected a view of the woods, scaled down to a tenth of the size.

The men locked their minds together over the scene, they searched the area for a hidden wavelength.

They scanned and searched every inch of the wooded area; they flushed out birds, rabbits, bugs, snakes and burrows of small animals, and miscellaneous rusted hand tools. They repeated the process across the area once again and discovered an area that wavered slightly.

Pay dirt!

The two servants concentrated deeply, probing intensely, and put all their effort into breaking the barrier.

Their master was beyond this point, somewhere.

Preston and Spencer concentrated on this spot and focused their strength into finding exactly where Mark was and what he was up against.

Chapter 14

Alma jumped up too fast and smashed her head into the roof of the low room. She immediately adjusted her posture while rubbing the top of her head, cursing under her breath.

"Bejion, we're leaving here, right now. Is there anything you want to take with you?" she asked the decrepit old man.

"Leaving now?" he asked. He blinked and looked around the room.

"Yes, leaving now. Don't worry, you have another life to live, a happier life. Everything will work out," she said, trying to ease his pain.

She determined from the setup, he had made this place his life. Alma could understand his reluctance to leave behind what was familiar, to begin another existence in plush surroundings, if he could make the comparison.

Bejion reached out and snatched the tin cup and gripped it to his chest with an expression of reverence. As he looked around the low-ceilinged room, a tear rolled over his eyelid, streaming down his dusty cheek.

With her eyes misting, she reached out with her right hand clasping her fingers through his and drew him toward her.

"Stand by my side, Bejion," she coaxed the little man as if he were a child.

He shuffled up to her, then turned his head to observe her. She closed her eyes and summoned her great powers. Within minutes, they were both transformed into glittering masses, then they vanished from the desolate room beneath the cells of the prison, leaving Ecko behind forever.

Will something direct me where to go?

She looked to the dense heavens around her. Which one is it? There's so many huge balls to choose from.

Planets, stars or moons, she couldn't tell one from the other. So many colors from up here. For some reason, she had expected everything in outer space to be in black and white, but she didn't know where that idea came from.

The black, cold universe, alive with colorful obstructions, whizzed past the two travelers. Broken down into molecular substructure, nothing could harm them. They passed through everything.

"There! There's Kredo," Bejion said, nodding toward a large planet.

She stared at the huge mass ahead and was suddenly apprehensive. What was she supposed to do? Stroll in and say, *Hi, Dad, how's life been treating you?*

Tremendous mixed feelings of love, fright, resentment and hate battled for first place. She was excited and nervous to meet her father.

So many years had passed. She strongly perceived the absence of her mother and denied herself the emotion of loss. She had to keep her head clear; too much was at stake.

The trip from Ecko to Kredo was almost instantaneous; zipping through space at twice the speed of snapping one's fingers. An instinctive intuition, perhaps from infancy, guided her to Cralic Sector.

They silently materialized in a familiar room.

A tall, gray-haired man in a long black robe with strange, intricate designs in turquoise beads and gold braids, stood gazing out of a large simulated window.

His back faced Alma and Bejion. Sensing he was not alone anymore, he turned slowly to witness the transformation of the two travelers into solid matter.

Guards appeared, as if out of thin air, to protect their ruler, ready to strike at the intruders.

Jetron frowned then held his hand up, stopping the rush of his men. Surely his eyes betrayed him as he gazed upon the familiar image.

"Xidiea? Xidiea!! My daughter!" Jetron exclaimed, questioning what his eyes claimed. He regained his mobility and rushed across the room to greet her.

"Father? Oh father!" was all she could say as she met him, arms outstretched.

They came together in a fierce hug, emotions clambering to the surface after so many years of separation. The silence lingered as they embraced their losses and newfound gains.

Tears swelled to flowing rivers in Alma's eyes, releasing the dam of pent-up emotions from the past few weeks.

A kaleidoscope of scenes from her life rushed through her mind.

Jetron observed the commotion and understood her turmoil. He dismissed the guards as he held his daughter tightly while silently condemning himself for her losses.

Moments later, he held her at arms-length to sweep his eyes over her.

Just like Reena! His beautiful wife lived again in his daughter. How proud she would have been! Tall, stately, her beautiful face so like his Reena's. Even the shape of her eyebrows and the prominent cheekbones were close reminders of the love he had lost.

Jetron observed her disheveled appearance. Her hands, face, arms and feet were dirty with scrapes and cuts. Her clothes were filthy. "What happened to you? Where have you been?" He summoned someone mentally.

A woman appeared with a garment over her arm.

"Xidiea, take a moment and go with Gynetta so she can help you get cleaned up," Jetron said. "Wait! Who is this with you?" He spotted the hunched, grimy man waiting dutifully where Alma had left him.

"Oh! I almost forgot! Father, you are in for a great shock. You remember Bejion, don't you? Asedi kidnapped him, thinking he could get information out of him and took him to Ecko. He played dead so they wouldn't implant the disc in his head, but he couldn't project to Kredo to tell you where he was.

"He's been crawling around in a network of tunnels all these years. That's why he can't stand up straight. I brought him back home," she said in a non-stop nervous chatter, sweeping an arm toward the man. "I hope you can help him. He's in pretty bad shape."

"Bejion? After all these years!" Jetron said. He left his daughter and crossed the room to the dirty little man. His servant was stooped over from the rough years of survival and miles of scurrying through tunnels.

Gynetta led Alma through a door to what Alma considered a Kredon equivalent of a bathroom. Gynetta hung the dress on a hook on the wall as Alma examined the room.

There was a large glassed-in room devoid of fixtures. A secluded area housed what looked like a toilet, and another area with a large round sink with a faucet.

Several shelves contained different sized and colored towels, and beautiful glass bottles which Alma assumed contained shampoo and soap.

"This is the bathing room," Gynetta said. "Just walk inside the stall and the water will spray."

"Do I take one of these bottles with me?" Alma asked.

"You will find a shelf of different bottles inside," Gynetta said. "There are products to clean your hair and body."

Alma looked at the glassed room again. "I don't see the shelf."

Gynetta held her hand to her mouth to stifle a laugh. "Oh my, you have never used the bathing room. I understand now. When you walk into the middle of the room the sensors will detect you. The shelf will extend from the wall and the water will spray. When you're finished, just step from the center to any of the sides and the water will stop and the shelf will retract."

Alma's mouth went slack. "That's incredible. I'm going to need two towels. One to wipe off with and one for my hair."

Jetron balanced on his toes. "Get comfortable, man," he said to his old friend and confidant. He took the mans leathered hands in his own and pulled him down to a more comfortable position.

"Well, old man, do you remember me?" Jetron asked.

Bejion's eyes skittered around the room. He frowned as he gazed on Jetron's face.

"Is that a new window, Jetron?"

"Yes, it is, my friend. You'll find quite a few new things around the complex. Do you remember your friend, Cordro? He's still here. Would you like to see him?" Jetron asked.

"My friend Cordro? We grew up together," Bejion remembered.

"Yes, you did. He grieved for you when we couldn't find you. Cordro will be happy to have his best friend back, just as I am," Jetron said. "Sit and relax for a few minutes while I summon him."

Alma joined the two men and sat on the floor with her legs crossed.

"What's wrong, Xidiea? You shouldn't have come by yourself; Hemlon should be by your side. Are you two having a difference of opinion you cannot work out?" Jetron asked.

"I understood everything had worked out beautifully between the two of you. My advisors reported on your beautiful wedding; the Earth customs of marriage ceremonies sound lovely, but it's a shame that most of those marriages aren't bonded together stronger," Jetron stated.

"You aren't experienced enough to come this far alone, although I can't argue the fact you arrived here unharmed."

"The wedding was lovely, Father. But now there's an emergency situation. Asedi has kidnapped my sons, and Mark—I mean Hemlon—is trapped somewhere, but I can't find him. Spencer and Preston are searching for him in the woods by the house."

"Kidnapped my grandsons? Why take two small boys when he could have taken you? That makes little sense at all. The man has clearly gone insane. I'll kill that vile beast when I find him!" Jetron thundered.

Alma drew in a deep breath. "I'm pretty sure Asedi didn't take Mark to the same place he brought the boys. Their combined power would most likely be too strong for him to control.

"I went to Ecko because I thought for sure Asedi had taken the boys there. That's when I found Bejion. He has a whole network of tunnels underneath the cells. Anyway, just before we left, I had a vision of the boys, then of Mark—Hemlon," she said, trying to fit the unfamiliar name into place.

"Hemlon was right, I should have put Asedi to death instead of banishing him." Jetron stood and paced.

"The people need someone strong to lead them. Since your mother died I have become distant, too introspective. It's been difficult for you, too, hasn't it Xidiea? Even your name sounds strange to you, doesn't it?" Compassion filled Jetron at that minute, making the weight more difficult to bear.

"You and mother did what you considered was best at the time," she said, a note of sadness creeping into her voice.

"The most difficult part was the lack of family. Everyone else I grew up with had aunts, uncles, grandparents and cousins. All I had were two people on the whole planet. I never had that strong bonding of family.

"Oh, well, it's all in here somewhere. I just haven't found all the pieces yet to put my heritage together."

"You've grown into a beautiful woman. Hemlon tells me you are learning increasingly more each day. Soon you will be ready to step into my shoes and give your old father a rest," he said, rubbing her back.

Turning to Bejion Jetron said, "And what are we to do with you, my old friend? I'm glad you're alive. I've missed your friendship over the years."

"Bejion used to be my sounding block. That's why Asedi stole him, I guess, thinking he could pry information out of him. Evidently, he didn't get any because he took all these long years to find you on Earth." Jetron said, turning toward his daughter.

A servant entered the room, having been silently summoned by his master. "Cordro, guess who this is?"

Cordro stared at the hunched-over old man.

"It's Bejion! Xidiea found him on Ecko and brought him home. Take him to the healer then return here."

"Bejion?" A shocked expression crossed the servant's face at the mention of his friend. Both men were the same age, and at one time, the same size.

Now, Cordro looked upon his friend aghast, not believing the rickety old man in the tattered, dirty clothes could possibly be the missing confidant that his master had searched for.

They had given up after months of combing the planet, thinking he had been killed.

Cordro stooped down and helped his friend to his feet. He walked beside him, one arm across Bejion's shoulder.

"Welcome home, my dear, dear friend. Let's put you back together again like you were thirty years ago," he whispered into Bejion's ear as he led him out of the door.

"I remember you. You're my best friend," Bejion said as they walked away. "Are you still my friend?"

Choked for words, Cordro hugged his friend. The two talked as they moved down the corridor.

"What will happen to him, Father?" Alma asked as she and her father stood up and walked to a padded bench along one wall. "He is cunning and alert one minute, then rambling and senile the next."

"He will be all right. The healer will make him whole again, you'll see. Perhaps his cortex has degenerated. It's of no matter; we can repair the damage. Cell reproduction methods are a simple task. Let's discuss more urgent matters. What did you see in the visions?" Jetron asked as he and Alma sat down.

"There was a symbol, or crest on the wall of this stately looking room. At first, I wondered if it was someplace in Cralic Sector, but I don't think so now. I've seen it before, maybe from the books I've been reading about Kredon history. Do you have a piece of paper and a pencil? I can sketch the room," she said.

"No need for that, my dear. Re-create the whole scene in your head as it appeared before you, and I'll see everything through your eyes," Jetron said.

"Don't worry Xidiea. I understand the difficulty of converting your thoughts because of the barbaric way you were raised. That was the worst mistake your mother, and I had ever made and I wish I could relive those years and change everything. Perhaps your mother would still be alive now."

"How can you do that though? I'm sure that the knowledge is in here someplace," she said tapping her forehead. "When will it ever surface?"

"My dear, something you should begin with is to understand the Spirit and the Universe are One, and that is the driving force of all life," Jetron explained.

"Everyone has these abilities; some are dormant from many centuries of non-use because of various stages of either religious or political influence. Earth is redeveloping, getting into the New Age, as they are calling it. It will be a full century before the New Age is accepted as the norm," he said.

"You must be careful and not slip up in front of anyone when you return to Earth. Your powers would be misunderstood by the present society."

"Let's do this thing. I want to see how it works," she said, eager to gain more understanding of her stolen life.

Taking only a minute, Alma re-created each vision.

Jetron concentrated and focused into his daughter's eyes. Beyond the green irises and black pupils, he viewed and heard everything that Alma had tried to explain to him.

"Hmm. Where have I seen that crest?" Jetron frowned, wracking his mind. "Let's go see PRETOR and find out if she knows anything about this."

"Who's Pretor, father?" Alma asked thinking of an ancient witch with white hair, a crooked, long nose and flowing robes.

"Where did you get that imagination?" he joked, glimpsing her witch image.

Alma smirked; she didn't have an answer.

"Lesson number one: PRETOR is the most sophisticated Comitol," he answered. He saw her confusion and explained in detail. "PRETOR means Probe Resisting, Eternally Testing, Objective Receiver; a Comitol is a computerized investigative tool."

"Oh!" she said, finally understanding.

They left the room and walked into an immense adjoining room, stark white, almost blinding Alma. After her eyes adjusted to the color, she took a sweeping look at the sterile room. A large white console dominated the entire center and was surrounded by unusual floating chairs that had control panels on each arm.

Jetron led Alma to one of the chairs and motioned for her to sit as he pushed the top left button on the right arm of his chair.

A probe popped up from the console in front of her. It looked like a giant slanted eye, about one foot across and three inches around. Immediately she remembered the Martians in the movie, *War of the Worlds*.

She opened her mouth to ask her father about her absurd preoccupation with the movie and shook her head and decided against it. A niggling in her head told her she wasn't too off track in her thinking PRETOR had made her movie debut.

"Show the probe your vision," Jetron encouraged.

She fidgeted while the probe identified her through retina patterns stored away when she was a baby.

"Xidiea, daughter of Reena and Jetron. Identification authenticated," PRETOR announced.

Alma was uncomfortable as the thing swayed, then inched forward, stopping close to her nose. She thought she would go cross-eyed if she tried to watch it.

She sensed that it was ready and played the scenes through her head, unblinking. When the vision ended, the probe immediately withdrew and sank into its fixture.

Alma was stunned as she glanced at the smooth console top that didn't show a trace of an opening of any kind.

"What's it doing?" she asked, amazed.

"It's searching for a match of anything it detected in your vision," Jetron told her.

"How long will it take?" she asked.

"It could be minutes or hours, depending upon how deep it has to go into its archives. PRETOR knows no boundaries and will keep searching until every resource is exhausted," Jetron said.

"Since I seem to remember that crest from somewhere, I'm sure it's recorded. My memory may fail me, but PRETOR's won't; our entire history is archived away."

"How could I have lived on Earth in an upcoming computer literate society and not realized that I was different? It doesn't make sense. Why didn't these hidden bits of information surface from being around similar things?" she asked.

"It wasn't meant to be, Xidiea. Those hidden bits of information were buried deep, well insulated to prevent anyone from finding out your true identity. They are being released slowly from a few keywords that Hemlon planted deep in your subconscious," Jetron said.

Alma met her father's eyes. She saw that he struggled as much as she did with the lost years and knowledge.

"Soon all these new things you are learning every minute of every day will become commonplace. I realize it is difficult for you to be patient, but it's all you can do at this point," he said.

"Are you hungry, Xidiea? We may have a long wait and I'm sure you haven't eaten in hours. It's important for you to keep your strength up because you have to balance both existences with your mind."

"Yes, I am rather hungry. I didn't think I'd have to eat while in this form but sensations like hunger, persist. You wouldn't happen to have a cheeseburger, would you?" she asked her father.

"Explain what a cheeseburger is. Perhaps we have something like that here. Was that one of your favorite foods on Earth?" he asked, trying to discover something about his daughter.

"It's a popular food served at what's called a fast food restaurant and classified as 'junk food'," she said.

"It's actually ground beef, from a cow. It's formed into a thin circular shape, called a 'patty,' which is cooked on a grill or in a pan. Most people top their burger with a slice of processed cheese, then put it on a hamburger bun," she explained.

Upon seeing her father's confusion, she patted his arm. "Anything will do."

They left the sterile-looking room and walked down a hallway, turning into an open doorway on the left.

This space reminded Alma of a lunchroom she had seen in a science fiction movie, with panels on the wall offering an assortment of food items and beverages.

A monitor displayed lists of available items and gave written instructions to the user, along with a three-dimensional picture of each item that looked so real her mouth watered.

As she scanned the contents, her hunger grew. She made up her mind and pushed the corresponding buttons, picked up a tray and waited for her choices to appear in the proper slots of the machine. She was rewarded in minutes and was surprised that the food looked just like the pictures she made her choices from.

Too bad cooking on Earth wasn't as easy; the food never looked like the pictures unless you were a pro with gourmet cooking classes to fall back on.

They moved from the vending-type machines to an octagonal-shaped white table surface that seemed to be suspended in the air. Matching legless chairs were also suspended.

Alma skeptically observed as her father placed his tray on the table and slid onto the chair. He pressed two different buttons on a control panel on the left arm.

The chair adjusted to his body and fit close to the table allowing him to eat in comfort.

Alma approached the table and placed her tray on the surface across from her father and eyed the chair. It was too high off the ground for her.

"Press the second button," Jetron said. "The one that shows a chair and a down arrow."

She scanned the panel, found the icon and pushed the button. The chair lowered several inches. Alma sat down and the chair rose and immediately glided closer to the table.

Another control panel was on the edge of the table and she recognized some of the symbols to raise or lower the table; she didn't know what the others were for and decided it wasn't important enough to worry about.

Timid with all the newness of the technology, she decided that observing was better than experimenting and wouldn't get her into trouble.

Utensils resembling forks and knives were the tools for eating. She picked up her fork and sampled the food. The aroma and taste of the meat was similar to beef.

The steaming accompaniment, which Alma figured was a vegetable, tasted like ripe gouda cheese, which she did not like at all. She forced down the mouthful with a grimace and took a sparing sip from the metal chalice and washed the bad taste from her mouth.

The liquid tasted like sparkling water, which was acceptable to her palate.

As she and her father ate, three demanding beeps sounded from the table control panel. Then a small modular screen lowered from the ceiling to rest in midair in front of Jetron. He frowned and scanned the information on the monitor.

"There's a bit of a problem," he said. "We've got conflicting information because PRETOR shows that the guards and the crest are of the planet Ndai, but that civilization has been dead for quite some time.

"I know for a fact that the planet is deserted because scientific teams test the air and surface from time to time. It will be another two centuries before we can do any experimental growing or life tests. The poisons in the air won't allow for anything to survive there," he said, adjusting his chair, then standing.

"We need to begin a search. There are many places where they could be."

Alma watched her father's lead and fumbled with the panel on her chair, not quite adjusting the height correctly. She had to ease off the edge of the chair until her toes touched the ground. It would definitely take practice.

They left the lunchroom and returned to the white room that housed PRETOR. Jetron sat in one of the control chairs and summoned the scanner. The large, slanted eye appeared at once.

"PRETOR, recall the vision you received from Xidiea," Jetron commanded.

Instantly, holographic scenes appeared.

"Send this information, along with the message I am about to give you, to all the ganji. Direct them to search the entire surface of the planet and report back to me as soon as they complete their mission.

"Record message: Using depth scans, search for the young male humans you see in this vision. Identify with eye probe. Search for the crest you see on the wall. Report any similarities. Take no action. Identify guards. Report any similarities. Take no action. That is all."

"You have Cody and Jamie's retina signatures?" she asked.

"Yes, Hemlon updated them from birth to the first birthday," Jetron said. He pushed another button on the control panel and the eye probe disappeared.

"What's a ganji?" Alma asked.

"I believe they're similar to police on Earth. Kredo uses robotic units. We don't have to worry about bribery, or any of the many other downfalls brought on by society. They are programmed to do a specific thing, and they carry out their duties to the letter. PRETOR is the only thing that can bring about changes to a ganji, and there are only a handful of people who can change PRETOR's programming," he explained.

"The eye scans were implemented around two hundred years ago," he explained. "We used to use fingerprints but discovered that they were too easy to change.

"Eyes, on the other hand, are unique in the retina patterns and no one will try to alter them as they would a fingerprint. One mistake, no matter how minor, could leave you blind."

"What about corrective surgery?" Alma asked. "People on Earth are having vision surgery to correct farsightedness, cataracts, nearsightedness and other things."

"When a replacement or repair is necessary, the adjustments are made in PRETOR's files and life goes on. Even Earth law enforcement professionals know a hardened criminal would use acid to erase or change the patterns on his fingers.

"Who do you know would be foolish enough to alter a retina? It's an infallible system, one Earth should consider," Jetron stated.

"Can you show me what a ganji looks like?" Alma asked. The word was curious.

"Of course," Jetron said as he pushed another button on the panel. A large screen popped up in the center of the white table. "Display ganji," Jetron commanded.

A clear vision appeared.

Alma expected to see *Darth Vader*-type robots and was disappointed at the sight on the screen. Small orbs of a bluish silver color hovered in the air and were approximately three inches in diameter, smooth and seamless to the eye.

"Oh!" she exclaimed. "They aren't what I pictured they'd be."

"You can't hide a man-type robot, and those models can be pretty clumsy even with all the technological advances we've made. Then there's the problem of agility; they can only be so quick and there's a problem of them being overtaken," Jetron said, understanding her disappointment.

"These units are the most sophisticated and come in all configurations, are cheap to build, and easy to maintain. We have thousands of them in each size," he said.

"As long as they get the job done I guess it doesn't matter what they look like," she conceded. "How long will it take for them to conduct their search?"

"Less than an Earth hour," he replied. "Kredon time is divided into kendahs; our days are much longer than your Earth periods and once you are permanently living here, you will adjust to the time difference. Even simple things like measures are different and will require converting figures in your mind, but it won't be difficult once it all comes together. You have that information stored in your subconscious. Sort through it and learn for the future."

Alma flinched. She raised her hand to her forehead and closed her eyes, trying to capture the vision that had flashed in front of her. Fragment flashes of scenes rushed past like a hallucinogenic trip from a bad drug overdose. Within seconds, her brain assimilated the pieces, and she put the scenes together. The effort drained her energy.

Jetron witnessed her expression of pain. He jumped from his chair and placed one of his arms around her waist and guided her to sit. "What is it, Xidiea?" he asked, alarmed.

"Someone is trying to break through the barrier surrounding the boys," she said weakly. Nausea crept up on her.

"Can you stop them?" Jetron asked, controlling his feelings so he wouldn't throw her off track.

"I don't know. I'll try," she whispered. She opened her eyes and stared ahead, not focusing on anything in the room. "Jamie. Cody. Can you hear me?" she whispered.

"Mom, where are you? I can't see you," Cody said.

"Don't be scared, Cody. They are trying to use fright to get you to lower your shield. I want you and Jamie to combine your power; concentrate hard. Make a double shield. You can do it, Cody, your father taught you how," she urged as she watched them.

The boys clenched each other's hands and squeezed their eyes shut. Passing words back and forth, Cody instructed his brother to think a fortress around them that was invincible.

"Think something that the Super Heroes can't even get into," Cody whispered.

Jamie smiled devilishly and started with his brother's request.

"You've succeeded, Cody. That's good. They won't be able to break through that barrier. Have they said anything about where you are?" she asked.

"No, they hardly ever say anything at all, but that man over by the drapes has a real weak mind because I can see his thoughts sometimes. When are you going to get here, Mom?" he asked, impatient.

"Soon, I hope. We're still trying to find out where they are hiding you. Which man, Cody?" she asked.

"The one to the left of that first window," he said.

"Take care of your little brother and keep that shield up. Remember, they might try to trick you, so use all the things you father taught you," she warned.

"He must have let his shield down temporarily when Cody stumbled upon it, because I can't get through," Jetron said.

"Damn! I'd like to blast his brains right out of his head! How can I be so close and yet so helpless? I can't stand it," she said as the scene faded.

With emotions storming, Alma and Jetron waited in dismal silence for the ganji to report back to PRETOR. Minutes passed into a half hour; Jetron paced the length of the sterile looking room.

BEEP! BEEP! BEEP!

Private musings were invaded by the demanding signal from PRETOR's spotless surface. Instantly, a monitor popped up out of the camouflaged interior and swung around to face Alma and Jetron.

"The search has ended with no success or similarities," a soft-spoken, female voice announced. "I am waiting for further instructions."

Jetron rested his chin in his hand. After several minutes, he approached a chair and seated himself, reaching for the control panel and pushing several buttons.

"PRETOR, send message modules throughout the galaxy. Seek information regarding Asedi, plus the vision provided by Xidiea. Check for similarities. Take no action."

"Why does PRETOR have a woman's voice?" Alma asked. "I was expecting a robotic sounding voice, you know, a hollow, synthesized projection. This is a surprise."

"PRETOR went through a sex change about 40 years ago," Jetron joked. "She used to have a male voice, but it was irritating to listen to, so we changed it. The only problem we have now is that she's been so finely programmed that she's annoying at times."

"What do you mean?" Alma asked.

"She likes to talk; when you want a direct answer, she gives a sermon. When she knows you're upset, she tries to comfort you, but she doesn't have the right responses so she gets you even more upset."

"Why haven't your programmers made the adjustments?" Alma asked. "Surely it's simple with your technology?"

"Yes, it's something I'll have attended to as soon as we are finished with this sordid task," Jetron said.

Another long stretch of silence filled the room. As Jetron paced, Alma glanced around quietly for a few minutes then leaned back in the chair and closed her eyes.

Within seconds, she was dozing. Visions filled the void under her closed eyes. First Asedi, then the boys.

A foggy picture of Mark flashed past, then suddenly her whole head filled with an unknown face chiseled from ice.

Alma jerked upright and covered her eyes with her hands. The face loomed inside her head, silently seeking something.

She gathered her wits and calmed the storm of her emotions and stared at the remarkable face. No communication passed between them; within minutes, her head was clear, and the face vanished.

"I can't stay here and wait, Father. I have to keep searching for my sons. Mark is still trapped somewhere—I can sense his helplessness and we can't do anything about it. If only Spencer and Preston could get to him. I need him, now!" she exclaimed, not sharing her new experience with her father.

"Xidiea, I know that nothing can console you, and I understand, but you must be careful not to fall into a trap. Asedi does not reason; he is long past sanity and is dangerous. He would welcome the chance of capturing you," Jetron said.

"But what is the point of all this?" Alma asked.

"We don't know what he wants of you, whether he wants to try to control you, or if he wants to kill you. I don't think he even knows what he wants—he's so far over the edge that nothing makes sense anymore," Jetron said.

"Father, I can't wait around for something else to happen," Alma said.

"Yes, I can see your determination," Jetron said. "If you must go, I want to send some ganji units with you—several minuscule models that will transmit information into PRE-TOR in case you uncover something."

"Will Asedi be able to detect them?" she asked.

"Possibly, but by the time he thinks of it, they will have transmitted what they learn from being near you," he told her.

"All right, but I want to leave now. How long will this take?" she asked.

Jetron walked to the controls and pushed a button. Alma paid attention as a tiny slot opened and closed on the console.

She waited patiently to see the ganji that her father wished to accompany her on the perilous journey, but she didn't see anything.

"Is there a problem?" she asked.

"No, everything is in order," he said.

"Where are they?" she asked, chafed.

"There's six buzzing around you at this very minute," Jetron said. "Come over here and look at the scanner."

She approached the chair and looked at the screen over his shoulder. Her image displayed graphically in a three-dimensional form surrounded by the tiny, luminous spheres.

"Incredible! They're so tiny! The scientific development in this society is unbelievable! Well, now that I have company, I'll continue my search."

"Be careful, Xidiea," Jetron said as he stood and hugged her.

"I will, Father," she said as she walked away, vanishing within minutes.

Chapter 15

In the dark, silent void of space, beyond the atmosphere of Kredo, the immense stage of the galaxy supported Alma. She floated in timelessness.

Eyes closed, her chin stretched toward the heavens. Her mind sought direction from the powers within her.

Crystalline in appearance, an awesome spectacle that few could claim to do. Long hair drifted out around her like bursts from a sun.

Centuries ago, Earth would have captured her image as a myth. They would have preserved her actions for all eternity on walls of caves and scrolls of parchment.

Where were those gods from Earth's past, she wondered? Which part of the heavens had they drifted off to when they abandoned the mortals of Earth? Why weren't they there to give her guidance?

She forced herself to be disciplined. Alma cleared her mind of all the useless nagging and chatter so she could grasp the knowledge seeping into her conscious mind. Mark had provided volumes of data.

Two bright green eyes shot open as the information she had been seeking about her sons surfaced.

She calculated her direction and headed for Neverron, a small, desolate planet neighboring Kredo.

Abandoned several years ago by zercite mining crews, gray, dusty soil blew wild in the roaring winds.

Lightning flashed and clouds rolled and gathered in the purple sky, threatening to punish the naked land.

All that remained on the surface were a few crumbling buildings and several covered mine shaft entrances.

When the need for more underground buildings arose, the planet would bustle with activity once again.

Alma stood on the barren surface with hair flying in the angered wind. She sent feelers out with her senses.

An awareness passed through her mind; she perceived something of Jamie and Cody but it was beyond her grasp. With something like sonar in her mind, Alma headed for one of the sheltered entrances.

Sand had drifted in piles in the open doorway. Nothing seemed disturbed by the activity of the inhabitants.

As she explored the place with her mind, the wind whipped the loose sand in a blanket of dust. As she brushed the film off her face, a stinging sensation inflamed her cheeks, then her neck, hands and feet.

Alma stared down at her hands and gasped in horror at the grayish brown lump on her right hand. She beat it off and discovered a purplish bruise and a trickle of blood.

Alma screamed and beat at the various parts of her body, terrified of the ordeal she was going through. A download hammered into her brain: Sand leech, non-poisonous.

When she was free of the infestation, she shrouded herself against the environment, not caring to relive the experience. Still, she pressed on.

A nagging, evasive sense guided her down the wide, dusty stairs to the mining level below. Old, stale dust, such as that found in a closed-up attic assailed her.

She saw several leeches fall to the ground, unable to penetrate the shield and hold on to her.

Alma searched for information in the depths of her mind and discovered what she sought.

Zercite, a precious metal abundant on Neverron, was extracted from the soil and stored in the underground vaults, then shipped to Kredo as needed.

The planet was mined for its only important resource, then left to the storming winds of the atmospheric wars in its development. Kredons deserted the planet until another trip for the mineral was necessary.

Another piece of information flitted across her mind: Beware of krodas. She tried to force the information but drew a blank as to the identity of the creature.

The bowels of the mine were dark and dry, almost too dry to breathe with all the dust. She stood on the bottom stair and her eyes adjusted to the surroundings.

Nothing was visible even as her eyes grew accustomed to the dark interior.

Alma mentally touched the gloomy place with her senses. She determined that the lighting fixtures had been left behind by the mining crews. Not understanding what she should do, she stood quietly as the energy in her mind undulated, waiting for a sign.

Something like a formula came forward. She translated the data and grasped the instructions.

"Light!" she rasped. She drew in a ragged breath from expending her power.

The neglected filaments of old wall lanterns glowed, straining within the orbs from the energy Alma produced. She used her newfound sensory skills and detected the ganji close by and wondered about them.

More of the buried power was seeping into her conscious mind with every minute, flooding her with knowledge. Soon she would assimilate the information and understand herself, her people, and the power surging inside of her. The picture would become complete.

She stepped onto the littered floor and walked down the narrow corridor. Alma observed the open vaults on either side and a few closed doors that hid nothing.

The gray-hooded man appeared about twenty steps in front of her. His sharp features plain, even in the dim lighting.

Asedi.

Alma's blood boiled with rage as her control teetered. The air became cold around her.

Energy whipped the inert shadows into static electricity, causing her hair to fly out around her.

Energy crackled sparks off the walls of the corridor. Her dress rippled close to her body in the storm.

"Ha, ha, ha!" The maniacal laughter bounced off the crumbling walls around her. "I knew you would come. I planted the suggestion in your mind and pulled the string. You're just like a puppet. You didn't have brains enough to explore the possibilities that perhaps this was a trap."

"Where are my sons, old man?" she thundered, her voice echoing down the corridor, slamming into him with its power.

An instant of worry washed over Asedi. He shook it aside, basking in his foolish triumph. Her power was obvious, and he sensed it growing.

Jealousy gnawed through any reasoning he was capable of. He pushed the envy out of his mind and gripped onto the thought that he was in control; he had the prize, and he presumed she knew it.

"You should be careful not to anger me, my dear; your family would not appreciate it."

"Cut the childish games, Asedi. What have you done with my sons? What use are they to you? You would never win their confidence. Their father taught them well—they would never defect. Where is Mark?" she said, gritting her teeth, trying to keep rational.

"Mark! Earth has rotted your brain! *Hemlon* is resting, that is all," he cackled. "The boys are being entertained by a few loyal friends of mine," he said, enjoying his minute of glory.

"Tell them to lower their shield or I'll destroy Hemlon!" he demanded, his voice ugly once again.

"Your wishes will never be realized! You can't get near Jamie and Cody, and you can't afford to harm Mark. Don't anger ME, Asedi!" she said as she started forward.

She reached out with a fist, clenched the air and lifted her arm. Asedi was jerked off the ground. He struggled, his arms flaying at the invisible vise that gripped him and held him captive. He gulped air and almost gave up.

"NOW!" he screamed, petrified.

Four powerful hands grabbed and pinioned Alma as another pair thrust a heavy, tight fitting metal helmet upon her head, plunging her in darkness. With her power contained, Asedi plunged to the floor; he jumped up and took control of his plan.

"AAAHHHHH!" she screamed, trying to reach for the object on top of her head. The strong arms restrained her; she was powerless.

A weakness overcame her, and she realized that the helmet was enforced with keletheon, an energy-constraining material. Unless she could dislodge the headpiece, she would remain in a state of stupor.

"Lock her up! Don't let her out of your sight for a minute and do not remove that helmet. She is the most dangerous Kredon alive!" he enunciated. "I will return later."

Millions of molecules raced through the crystalline image in the corridor, then Asedi vanished, leaving the others behind.

"PRETOR, report your findings," Jetron commanded.

"There is nothing significant to report at this time," the feminine voice cooed. "I detect an increase in your blood pressure. Would you like me to monitor your vital statistics?"

"No, I don't want my vital statistics monitored. I know when I am upset! Check on the ganji and see if there are any visuals yet," Jetron snapped.

He slammed his hand on the surface. Worried about his daughter, he attacked PRETOR and his servants.

"Visuals are ready now," responded the lilting voice.

Jetron studied the screen in silence as he sat in the white chair, a sour look on his face. He watched as the screen came to life with a clear picture which fuzzed out momentarily, then became sharp once more.

The raging surface storm on Neverron was in full sight.

The scene shifted from the ganji who stayed posted outside, to another tiny orb inside the structure.

The feed picked up where Xidiea walked down the dusty stairs and used her energy to turn on the lights.

"Good. She's learning," he said as he watched her concentrated actions. In the next minute, his happiness disintegrated and anger shot through his veins as he recognized the intruder.

"Asedi!" he roared.

The more he watched, the angrier he became. When he witnessed the scuffle, he was furious, pounding his fist on the white surface with brute force.

"Did one of the ganji attach itself to Asedi?" he demanded.

"Contact has been made," the soft voice replied.

"Where is Xidiea now?" he asked, frenzied.

"The third planet in the system," PRETOR began.

"Just give me the name of the place!" Jetron fumed. "Is it one of our old mining colonies or someone else's?"

The three burly men carried out their master's task, making light conversation as they proceeded down the hall.

Two of the men carried Alma's limp body and one walked ahead to the small vault and opened the door.

They carefully laid her down on a platform in the center of the small, neglected room, mindful of not removing the crippling helmet.

"Dolru, stay in the room and guard the woman. Avril and I will scan the area for ganji," Oxor said.

Dolru nodded his dark head and closed the door. He stood in front of it, facing Alma. The small room was eight feet square, minimized immensely by the three by six platform.

A perfect example of what Mr. Universe should look like, Dolru's immense size overwhelmed the tiny room. As he stood gazing at Alma, emotions rushed through him. He noted how soft her skin looked; he longed to touch her.

Before enlisting in Asedi's army, Dolru had been tucked away on Ecko, rotting in a small cell due to a long chain of crimes. He had been lucky that the council had not voted for his brain to be restructured for menial tasks.

Dolru shook those unpleasant memories aside; after all, they hadn't done it, so he was safe as long as he played Asedi's game.

The man was crazy, wanting to be emperor of the universe. He figured that by freeing the prisoners on Ecko, he would gain their devout loyalty.

He'll not make a slave of me!

Dolru switched his attention to the lovely, mysterious woman.

Dolru heard many conversations about Jetron's daughter, but he never fully pieced together why she was here and what was so important.

The old Keeper gave no one a full view of his plan; he was jealous and suspicious of everyone and a menace to society, Dolru thought.

Not having an interest in politics, Dolru had spent most of his time dodging responsibilities and getting into trouble. He drank too much, fought over other men's women—those things had been his downfall more than once.

It had been many, many months since he had touched a woman. He had never been intimate with a woman of the upper class. He was used to the working women from the growing facilities or the food manufacturers.

Dolru had never been this close to royalty. He abandoned his post and strode over to the restrained woman and gazed at her face.

So lovely; such smooth unblemished skin.

Unbeknownst to him, she was expanding her mind, growing, going deeper inside herself since she was physically powerless.

Dolru got caught up in his emotions and fantasies as he brushed his hand up her arm, across her collarbone. Her skin was as soft as a baby's; he shivered with anticipation.

He licked his own thick lips and took the liberty of running his hand across her bosom then cupping her right breast.

His eyes gleamed with his desire, glazed with lust.

He's going to rape me!

She screamed inside her mind.

Alma clenched her teeth as she fought the keletheon trap; she had to get rid of the helmet to defend herself against the vile man.

She shuddered and raged internally as if her mind would explode when he rubbed his thumb against her nipple.

Ragged breaths escaped his wet lips as he kept plying her body with caresses. Dolru removed his helmet and placed it on the floor.

He eased himself up onto the platform, balancing precariously on the edge. He leaned over and covered one side of her body with his while he frantically cupped and squeezed her breasts and kissed her exposed skin.

She knew he was beyond the point of turning back. It was only a matter of time before he ripped her clothes off and straddled her.

He groaned as his lips moved to her left breast as he continued kneading her.

Dolru pushed aside the fabric and suckled her breast.

Alma stormed inside. She gathered all her energy together in a torrential funnel inside her inner mind and blasted it outward. Lightening quick, her hands shot up and knocked the helmet from her head.

She thrust him aside with a force that threw him against the far wall. Alma quickly slid off the platform and turned to face her enemy. The level of her fury was as clear as the air she breathed in ragged gulps.

Dolru lunged forward and attempted to grab Alma; she was his responsibility and he would have to pay the price if she were to escape. He would not let that happen; he could not afford to anger Asedi and chance going back to prison. Her expression frightened him.

"How dare you defile me!" She stared at him eye to eye, a look of pure wildness on her face. Not thinking rationally, she thrust her power inside his mind, blasting his brain, crumbling his senses—destroying him.

She had no pity for him as his mouth gaped and he slid to the floor, settling on his knees. He stared blankly, spittle drooling over his lips and down his chin, barely equal to the intelligence level of an infant.

Alma reined in her emotions and drew on her powers. She transported herself back toward Kredo. Her sons were not on Neverron. She didn't know where they were.

"Mark! Hemlon! Where are you? I need you!" she wailed into the galaxy, her arms outstretched. Despair overwhelmed her as she covered her eyes with her hands and sobbed, loud racking sounds. Only the heavens heard her cries of torment.

Chapter 16

Preston and Spencer probed deep, concentrating on a small area in the woods, and weakened the zone trap where their master was held captive.

"Let's go now. Conditions seem to be right," Preston whispered, fearing that any other noise or stray thought would break the contact.

"Yes, we can pass now," Spencer double-checked.

Preston observed everything around him with his powers. He nodded, eager to end the suspension. The vision of the wooded area disappeared, along with the two men. Minutes later they materialized in a strange, hidden zone.

"Is this the correct spot?" Spencer asked, his voice echoing into the foggy dampness of the strange zone. His brows creased as his eyes adjusted to the stark white place.

"Yes, I'm sure of it. Keep close by, this is an uncharted region and there may be pitfalls," Preston replied, echoing.

"I sense something near. Do you?" Spencer asked with apprehension.

"Yes, I do. It's master Mark," Preston said. "Is he here in this place, or beyond? I can't tell anymore."

"He's here," Spencer said with clarity. Abruptly, he stopped walking and talking and yanked Preston's arm to stop him.

Don't speak, move or make any type of aggressive move. Look into the fog.

He enunciated each word inside Preston's mind.

Preston scanned the area ahead and stiffened. He sucked in his breath as his mind investigated.

Beyond the rolling fog, directly in front of them was a giant fog figure.

Similar to what Jack Frost should look like if he were not a fable, the figure had a long, lean face. Ice-like long hair fell to below weak, narrow shoulders.

The robe-clad body was thin, standing still.

Piercing slate eyes watched them; one long, bony hand held a sleek, black staff, the other arm hung by his side. His two feet were shod in primitive looking leather sandals.

Project your shield. Preston said mentally. *He's going to act soon.*

Spencer nodded inside Preston's mind.

The figure moved his staff to a diagonal position, making his intentions clear. He expected them to stay put.

"What do you seek in Ruar?" his deep voice reverberated.

"We come in peace, searching for our master who was trapped here by an evil renegade," Spencer answered, his voice echoing strangely.

"You are not of the Earth world," the figure said knowingly.

"We are of Kredo," Spencer stated, intuitively knowing that he need not explain further.

"Your powers are strong together, but not as strong as the master that you seek," the strange being said.

"Yes, that is true. Will you lead us to him?" Preston asked. He determined the fog figure would not harm them.

"Your intentions are honorable; I cannot hold the Kredon for the purpose of evil. The other will be dealt with if he should choose to return here. Ruar is a peaceful zone, a place for superior intelligence and training. I am the guardian," he said, moving his staff slowly in front of him.

At that minute Mark appeared before them, laying on a foggy slab, in a state of stasis.

Alarmed, Preston and Spencer stared at him.

The fog figure waved his staff again, and Mark was released from the coma-like state of mind in which he had been held. Within minutes, he slowly sat up, rubbing the back of his neck, then he turned toward the fog figure and nodded his head in respect.

"What you seek is here," the being expounded, moving his arms. A vision of a planetary system appeared, then, more precisely, a remote moon was singled out.

"There are many traps waiting for you; evil seeks triumph and will succeed unless you are careful. Take this staff," he said, waving his staff in front of him.

A smaller version of the staff appeared on the foggy surface that Mark had vacated.

"The staff will guide and protect you. Hold it solidly in your hand and don't let go." The Guardian of Ruar wavered.

"Thank you for your help. I will return this to you when I am finished with my mission," Mark said as he picked up the staff.

"There is no need," the fog figure echoed then vanished.

The three stood still for a minute, looking around the area. It was hard to determine if this zone was made of solid matter or just fog. Even the place where they stood was a mystery.

All they could see was the rolling fog.

Everything was bright white and there was no way of determining whether they were in a chamber or suspended in air and clouds. They were not on anything solid.

"Let's go!" Preston said, shivering slightly. Mark and Spencer agreed; the three crystallized, then vanished. Minutes later, they appeared in the hidden room in the house in Houston.

"Be on your guard for trouble; warn Cook. If necessary, return to Cralic Sector, but above all else, protect my wife," Mark instructed.

"I suspect something is going to happen and no matter how well prepared we are, Asedi will take us by surprise and get through our barriers. We can't let anything happen to Alma's physical body," Mark said, then vanished.

Preston and Spencer lingered in the room digesting Mark's words. They mind-traced their master through space, making sure of his safe travels.

The Ruar staff wouldn't let harm through to him, they deduced through probing. Thick dread followed confidence as they pulled their minds back to Earth. The master's mission was urgent—he had to find his sons. Asedi was insane, dangerous, and would stop at nothing to accomplish his goals.

The pull of the staff led Mark through the vast darkness of space.

The Bef planetary system lay ahead, and suddenly he knew where he must go.

Ndai, the fifth planet from Bef's sun had been deserted since the middle of the last century and was at one time a corrupt world. The greed of the people caused their doom.

Pirate raiding ships from Ndai attacked other ships and planets. They returned home with a potent virus that spread across the surface of Ndai killing life rapidly.

Surely, some Ndaians had escaped the death? Mark suspected there were occupants on the Ndai moon and that the staff was leading him to the precise location of an evil horde.

Silently, he thanked the Guardian of Ruar; without his help, Mark would have had a futile search indeed.

The heavens were vast with many planetary systems, some inhabited, others developing.

It would have taken him weeks to compile a list of the suspect places to search, weeks he could not spare.

Zeber, the rocky moon, was suddenly in sight. Yes, he was sure there were Ndaians living there; he aimed to find out who was helping Asedi.

Curse them! Damn their evil hearts.

As the Ruar staff directed him over the surface, Mark scanned the passing terrain. Huge craters gouged the caramel-colored surface; only a small amount of water was in sight, surely not enough to sustain life forms known to him.

As he approached a colossal abyss, the staff pulled him down into the center of the crater. To his amazement, Mark discovered a civilization deep inside the huge pit.

A city was molded into the sides of the crater, ablaze with lights, teeming with human movement. He wondered how many other craters were developed. How clever, to build the city into the walls protected by the overhang; no one knew there was life on Zeber, and no one suspected surviving Ndaians.

Mark took in all the activity and wondered what other foul people lived here; the excrement of society, no doubt.

His journey slowed, approaching a large dwelling that must be the ruling party headquarters. Without warning, the staff stopped its journey, thrusting Mark to a stop.

He rubbed his aching arm from the force of exertion and winced as strained muscles tightened in a spasm.

Mark cursed silently at the unfortunate timing of a physical weakness. He shoved the ailment to the depths of his mind so it wouldn't interfere with his mission.

He stared at the entrance and let his mind wander room by room beyond the door. He came upon what he sought: His sons. He backed out and his mind rejoined his body.

The staff, he discovered, seemed to have a wisdom all of its own. It positioned itself vertically in front of him and urged him forward with a unique energy.

Mark walked through the thick door as if it weren't there. He continued through furnished rooms, devoid of people.

Passing a mirror, he noticed that there was no image of himself projected. He wondered what other powers the Ruar staff concealed.

Never before had he found another society as developed as his own people. He would like to learn more about Ruar when he returned to Earth.

Mark entered the room where the boys were surrounded by the guard—a test of his invisibility. He stood at the threshold of the room and expected to be pounced upon by the marauders, but no one made a move, or acknowledged his presence. Mark moved forward toward his sons.

The staff dipped forward momentarily then straightened, beckoning him to continue.

The shield allowed him passage, and he walked on, stopping directly behind the boys. Keeping his presence from the enemy, he spoke inside his sons' minds.

Be still and don't let on that I'm here; I am with you now, but you cannot see me. I have to find a way to cause a diversion so we can leave.

The boys relaxed.

Alma. Xidiea. The name flitted back and forth in her stressed mind as she journeyed back to Kredo. There was a place for each name as with Mark and Hemlon.

She wished her father would call her Alma, but he and her mother had named her Xidiea and that was how he thought of her.

The Earth name had been chosen by servants who had raised her from infancy on her foster planet. They made sure she fit into the life, thereby duplicating an average household.

Unfortunately, the natural love and affection of parents had been lacking. Mark made her aware of the missing remembrances of practically every household in America: photos of her parents.

The tragic story had not been questioned because she had no hint of anything being out of place. She had been educated, cultivated and groomed for normal Earth life. The Kredon information was buried deep in the servants' minds for fear of being found out.

Alma thought back to her early years. She remembered one instance when she had come upon her aunt and uncle unexpectedly when they must have been sending a message to Kredo. She recalled a strange box that must have been a transmitter and the explanation her aunt provided.

"Oh, your uncle found this old radio by the side of the road and he's trying to fix it. He used to work at the power plant before he retired, remember dear?"

Of course, she didn't remember! She had accepted the story as any young person had. Families assumed children remembered everyone and everything from generations past and present.

Resentment flooded through her.

Resentment for her hidden heritage. In her present state of mind, flooded with worry for her sons and husband, she balanced precariously on the edge of emotional insolvency.

She entered Cralic Sector and emerged close to PRETOR in the white room.

Her father stood nearby, lost in his memories. Upon noting her presence, he came forward and held out his arms; he sensed her feelings, awash in defeat.

At once, Jetron realized the problem: Her inner turmoil regarding the slight differences was compounded by all that had happened in the short span of time.

Jetron held her tight and tried to absorb her hurt as she sobbed.

"Don't dwell on the past; look toward the future and pave the way for my grandsons. They have much to learn and have to be prepared to step into your shoes when the time comes. They are young and will adapt much easier than you have. Let's check PRETOR and see if there are any reports," he said, comforting her.

Alma abruptly pulled away from him while tears streamed down her face.

All her hurt and anger poured forth and she couldn't stop it. "How could you and mother have abandoned me? You left me so vulnerable. I never knew a parent's love. I was raised with a skewed upbringing that denied me my heritage."

"Xidiea…" Jetron said.

"My name is Alma! You left me with strangers. They named me. And while I have to assimilate all the knowledge that Mark… Hemlon… poured into me, I'm not a whole person anymore. I'm lost!"

Urgent beeping sounds filled the room. "There must be visuals from the ganji," Jetron explained. He walked over to the console.

Alma stayed where she was for a moment, collecting her emotions. She finally joined him at the console.

Jetron slid into the closest chair and pushed several buttons. Alma watched over his shoulder as the monitor appeared and played a scene.

They saw Jamie and Cody in their protected shield surrounded by guards. Asedi stood close by, probably plotting. Alma closed her eyes and frowned.

"What is it?" Jetron asked.

"Mark's presence is near the boys," she said, confused.

As she stared at the monitor, she didn't see him. A ganji probe was still attached to Asedi, and another was monitoring the room from another location.

Expletives crowded Mark's mind as Asedi entered the room. He had hoped the old Keeper couldn't detect him while he was working out a diversion.

Sensing that Alma was at Cralic Sector, he knew what to do. He gathered his full energy and channeled his consciousness in her direction. She and Jetron could arrange a diversion.

"Father, Mark is there! We just can't see him. He needs a distraction so he and the boys can escape undetected. Can you have PRETOR make one of the ganji leave the room and do something?" she asked, her voice high, reflecting her turmoil.

"Hhmm. PRETOR, display total surroundings," Jetron commanded.

Rooms whizzed past quickly then the outside of the residence appeared. "Stop! Proceed forward, slowly," Jetron said to the machine. They saw the replay of Asedi going through the front door and various rooms until he came upon the room with the boys.

"Replay, slowly," Jetron said in a controlled voice. When the scene showed a room at the opposite end of the dwelling, Jetron stopped the film. "PRETOR, move one of the ganji to this location. Cause a diversion by having the ganji fire missiles at an insignificant object."

"Is this a defense tactic?" PRETOR's singsong voice questioned.

"No, this is a diversion. Leave scanners on. I wish to view," he said.

As Mark and the boys waited to escape, a loud explosion sounded nearby; the flash of a fireball lit the room. The guards took immediate action, running through the double doors with Asedi in the lead, barking out instructions.

"Quickly now, Cody, climb on my back and put your hands around my neck, but be careful that you don't choke me. Jamie, come here," Mark said, picking up his younger son and balancing him on his hip while he adjusted the staff in front of him.

The three blended into the air surrounding them. They left, passing through the wall and the outer bricks and clay, rushing through the atmosphere in a split second, streaking across the heavens.

"Destroy the ganji! You," Asedi screamed in a crazed voice, pointing to two soldiers, "Search the area for more ganji! Find them; destroy them; they are transmitting back to Cralic Sector!"

In a rush, he realized his mistake; he had left the two young boys unattended! He knew his prizes were gone before he ran into the room.

Asedi seethed beyond control as he returned to the outer room where the damage had been done. His anger was aimed inwardly because he knew that the ganji had attached to him when he returned from Neverron.

"Hemlon has been freed. This was not the work of Xidiea," he muttered. "They have had help from someone else!"

Chapter 17

N erves electrified, Alma had difficulty staying in one spot while her father watched events taking place on the godforsaken moon.

Some of Asedi's men were combating the fire before the whole structure burst into flames. Others scanned every room with a small, thin black box, searching for hidden ganji.

The tiny units were the most sophisticated versions, excellent at evasive sensory tactics. Asedi had no idea if he succeeded in destroying all the units that had attached to him when he left Neverron. Ganji were hard to detect.

Sick with apprehension, Alma wandered out of PRETOR's room and walked the short distance to a room with simulated windows.

Alma stood before a picture window scene of sunny fields of wildflowers swaying in a soft breeze. She recalled the peaceful life she had led as an unsuspecting Earthling.

Memories of trips to the zoo, museums, beautiful Rice University where she had taken the boys occasionally, came rushing to her mind. They pretended the Rice campus was a castle in a private kingdom and had played for hours while Alma had read a book or sat in the sun.

Where were those long-lost days? Damned if she hadn't been pulled into a nest of vipers!

Kredo should be a universal representation of peace and serenity. Instead, a maniac was running wild, destroying people.

As her anger rose, she spread her arms toward the full, simulated sun. Hurricane-force wind whirled around her, causing her long amber hair to waft out like grasping tentacles of a raging fire.

Static jumped and crackled around her, electrifying the room. As the storm of emotions continued, her mind soaked in everything. She digested every bit of information found in her subconscious, then searched for information surrounding her.

Her mind swallowed and digested knowledge as her strength grew, waiting to strike out at her enemy.

Jetron completed the session with PRETOR and sat quietly. He snapped out of his deep reverie and became aware he was alone.

A sound in the next room caught his attention.

Jetron was careful not to make a noise as he entered the room and caught the scene before him.

Instantly, he understood what was happening: His daughter was finally coming into her full power. She would be a formidable foe to anyone who dared cross her, but his instincts told him she would not abuse her powers.

Asedi was a different story. Jetron would not interfere; justice would be done. He saw the power grow inside her.

She was a new breed. For a fleeting moment, he worried about her inexperience; then he pushed that judgement aside. She would have to learn how to control it, he reckoned.

No one else equaled her intelligence or power. Hemlon came close, but she surpassed him. Could he control her? Did she need to be controlled? Many scenarios raced through his mind.

A section of the galaxy appeared on the window. Alma closed her eyes for an instant and found the place she was seeking and combed the area. She sought out Asedi on Zeber and projected a vision of him on the window in front of her.

"You cannot hide from me, evil one; you cannot escape your fate. The universe is mine and I shall not share it with you," she stated, her voice sounding hollow and strange.

"You have strayed and have accepted a life of corruption, bringing down everyone around you. Kredo doesn't want you; Earth doesn't want you; and I don't want you seeking others out to poison another society with your twisted plans."

"You have destroyed innocent people, my mother being one of them. I'm not giving you another chance to come after my sons, my husband, or even me. My father made a grave mistake many years ago when he let you live. I don't have that compassion for you. Your number is up!"

Fear washed across Asedi's face. He acquiesced; he was no competition for her powers. She had finally come into her own forces; there were no equals.

He should have found her when she was a child before Hemlon returned to her life. Now he feared that her sons possessed the same great powers. They had all known at her birth that she was beyond the level of intelligence of Kredon lords, past and present.

He should have destroyed her then or stolen her to direct her loyalty to him. Kredo had prided itself in having the most superior minds in the universe, and with Xidiea, the record remained unbroken.

Her birthing test reported an astounding sixty percent increased amount of intelligence capacity over her fellow Kredons.

Asedi looked around. The smoldering room couldn't hide him.

The Ndaians were a little upset at what had just taken place. Their secretive existence was out in the open, and enforcers would come. No, he would not be welcome. He had betrayed them with his sloppiness and over-anxious greed.

"You have what you want; your husband and sons are free. What more do you want?"

Perhaps she could be reasoned with?

"There will be no plea bargains, Asedi. I will hunt you down and feed you to the lions," she said. She thrust a picture of his fate in his mind—a scene of gladiators in the ring facing lions.

He shuddered.

Alma released the vision and turned toward her father. "I won't be still until that man no longer exists!"

Jetron walked to his daughter's side and placed a comforting arm across her shoulders. He drew her from the vivid window scene to one of the yellow padded benches along the wall. They sat facing each other and he took her hands in his own.

"You cannot let your emotions turn you inside out," Jetron said. "There must be a balance; you have to come to terms with yourself, or you will not be the type of ruler that your Kredon subjects need.

"You are not ready yet, Xidiea, but don't despair. Hemlon must teach you more. Although you have your full powers and you are stronger than any other, you do not have the full maturity to overcome spontaneous outbursts. That could be dangerous for our people."

Alma nodded her understanding. She bent her head, tears misting her eyes. She acknowledged what her father said was true; she was not ready to take over.

This one instance, her first experience with these matters had proven that she was not yet ready for the complexity of the ruling position. She couldn't afford to jump to a quick decision, millions of people depended upon her sound judgement.

"I'll learn, father. The answers are inside of me," she said, placing her hand on his. "Mark will guide me."

Feeling a presence in the otherwise deserted room, her head bobbed up instantly.

Seconds later, Mark and the boys appeared only feet away. They hadn't materialized in the familiar crystalline manner, but wholly.

Alma jumped to her feet. Mark carried a strange staff in one hand while balancing Jamie on one hip with Cody hanging onto his back.

"Mom!" they squealed in unison as they jumped down and ran across the room to their mother.

Alma caught Jamie in a run; she scooped him up and sank down on the bench as he darted onto her lap and squeezed her tight, while Cody hugged her neck. They did their best to compete to be heard, the noise level increased as each boy told his version of the adventure.

Mark placed the staff against the wall and observed the reunion quietly.

"I'm so glad you're both alright!" she said, returning their hugs. "Calm down and be quiet, you'll each get a chance to tell your stories. Right now, I want to introduce you to someone."

She presented Jamie and Cody to Jetron. "This is your grandfather, my father!" Alma said, making the introductions.

The boys went through a display of being shy, then curious, then accepting, as they began a riot of conversation with their newly-found relative.

Elated at finally seeing them in the flesh, Jetron hugged each of his grandsons. He took them by the hand and led them out of the room with a steady stream of conversation to distract them from their parents.

I'll leave you two in peace, he told them in the silent Kredon way.

Not wasting a minute, Alma and Mark raced into each other's arms in a crushing embrace. A rush of questions flowed from Alma

"I was so worried about you, where were you? Did Preston and Spencer help you? Where did you get that odd-looking staff? Were you hurt?"

"First things first," he said huskily. He lowered his handsome blond head and seared her lips with his own.

He captured her face in his hands and continued to mesmerize her senses with his sensual attack, while she clung to him, barely able to keep her knees from buckling. Mark's arms swept around her, drawing her to him, warming her. Alma let herself go with the heady feelings she was experiencing.

While continuing to ravish her mouth, Mark crept inside her mind, loving her. His lips moved seductively over hers, his tongue exploring the inside of her mouth, skillfully playing hide and seek with hers.

When they parted, Alma gasped for breath, almost drowning in the passion she was experiencing. Face flushed, lips swollen from the intense minute shared with Mark, she looked like a woman that had been made love to thoroughly and had enjoyed every minute of it.

"Priorities have been taken care of," she said demurely. She reluctantly pulled away from his warm body. "It's now time for ninety questions."

Mark retrieved the black staff and returned to Alma's side. "Are you familiar with the zone of Ruar that lies parallel to Earth's existence? That is where I was trapped when Spencer and Preston finally found where to search.

"Evidently, Asedi convinced the Guardian of Ruar that I was a dangerous criminal, and I needed to be restrained until he returned for me. The Guardian does not like being lied to. He will deal with Asedi if he should ever turn up there again."

"The Guardian loaned me this staff, Alma. I've never experienced anything like it before. The sheer power that this thing contains is remarkable, and the Guardian holds many secrets.

"I want to return there to discover more about the zone and who the Guardian is. I'm not sure if others live there, or what he is doing there," Mark said, engrossed with the mystery.

"Let me see it," she said, holding her hand near the shiny black staff. As Mark handed it to her, a loud, breathless gasp escaped her lips as her hand gripped the object.

"AAAHHH!" she yelled. Her eyes widened; an intense look crossed her face. Mark reached for the staff and was repelled with a fierce shove by an invisible energy force that threw him against the far wall.

He used all his power and failed to penetrate the barrier. Not even a wave of weakness—the force field was a device of Ruar—power and energy.

"EENNNERGGY!" she screamed through clenched teeth. "RRRUSHING THROUGH MY BODY. POOWERRFULLL!"

Alma drew ragged breaths, closing her eyes momentarily. Minutes later she opened her eyes.

"PRRETORRR!" she screamed.

Jetron entered the room and was momentarily stunned by what he witnessed. Immediately, he recovered his senses and took command of the situation.

"PRETOR, scan Xidiea and chart," he barked. A scanning eye popped out of a hidden ceiling unit and worked its way up, down, and around Alma's body, stopping close to the energized staff at several intervals. PRETOR was not repelled.

Alma gritted her teeth and rode out the tempest. As suddenly as it began, the force withdrew into the staff, leaving Alma breathless.

Mark rushed forward, reached out and caught Alma before she crumpled to the floor, dropping the strange black staff, which clattered loudly on the white tiled floor.

"Alma, are you alright?" Mark cried out.

"Yyeess," she said, teeth chattering.

"Xidiea! What happened?" Jetron asked, alarmed.

"It wasn't malicious. On the contrary, it was a gift of power and energy from the Guardian of Ruar," she whispered to the two stunned men.

Alma rested a minute, eyes closed as the tingling sensation continued to course through her fingers then she inhaled deeply and exhaled slowly.

"He knows more about you, Mark, than you do, and he learned about me through your subconscious. He has more knowledge than PRETOR could store in a lifetime," she ended, breathless.

"But why did this happen? What was the purpose of this *gift*?" Jetron asked.

"Because he thinks of me as an equal," she said quietly.

Both men stared at her, stunned. The implication was astounding. Was she the beginning of a whole new evolution of Kredons? Jetron and Mark locked her out of their minds and merged their minds in a silent conference.

Do we let this other outside race interfere, Jetron asked silently?

What about my sons? Mark asked.

Are we going to be faced with intelligence that we cannot cope with yet? Will we be able to channel this intelligence and educate it?

Neither had the answers.

Chapter 18

"Power is all around you, Alma," Mark said. "It's visible—so different from the Kredon power. Do you feel any different? Delve inside for the answer."

"It's as if a current is racing up and down my veins. Am I transparent? Do I appear different?" she asked.

I'm afraid to know. I'm afraid of what this has done to me. I was barely able to control my Kredon power—now this. What am I to do with it? Why me? I'm not the right person for all of this. This gift should go to Mark who is older and more knowledgeable.

"No, there's no difference. You're absorbing the Guardians charge of power and, I imagine, it will take time to find a place for it to settle," Jetron said.

"PRETOR, project your findings onto the window."

The weird scene unfolded before the three pairs of eyes. The holographic display pronounced the energy around Alma in an astounding new light; energy, shown in bright red, charged and bounced off her yellow body. The staff remained black.

"Are there any physical changes noted?" she asked PRETOR.

The machine replied "No."

"Any mental changes?" she probed.

"Your question cannot be answered at this time," the soft voice replied.

"Why can't you answer that question?" Jetron asked. He was afraid to hear this specific answer. Afraid what he and Mark had discussed silently was going to be verbalized, he didn't want to deal with the answer right now.

"I do not have adequate data to make a comparison," PRETOR answered.

Jetron, Mark, and Alma were confused by the machines response.

Mark tapped into Jetron's mind.

I think our fears have been realized. We must make plans, but I don't know what to plan for. Let us observe for a while and see what happens then call the high council together.

"That is all," Jetron said, dismissing the computer. The holographic scene on the screen was instantly replaced with the soothing field of colorful flowers swaying in a gentle breeze.

Alma turned away from the window and bent to pick up the black staff. It no longer threatened her—but seemed ordinary. A scene flashed through her mind then vanished.

"Is Bejion whole again, father?" she asked.

"Yes, I think the healer is finished. Do you want to see him?" Jetron asked.

"Yes. Asedi made several trips to Ecko, and since Bejion tunneled all over the prison, I'm sure he overheard many conversations. I tried to ask him on Ecko, but he couldn't lock onto an answer. I just hope he can remember and recite the right conversations," Alma said.

Silently, Jetron beckoned the man. Within minutes, a tall, handsome man in a brown cloak entered the room. "Yes, sire?" his educated voice softly questioned.

What a distinguished looking man.

Alma stared at the man opposite her father and wondered if this were the healer. He was about the same age as her parent, brown hair singed with silver shards, and an interesting face, lightly lined.

Soft brown eyes, a little saddened, looked at each person in the room, remembering.

"Bejion, it's so good to see you!" Jetron said, rejoiced.

"Bejion!" Alma gasped. "It can't be! Are you real?"

"Of course, he's real," Jetron exclaimed, laughing. "This is exactly the way he looked when you were born, except for a few lines here and there. It's as if he never left."

"How did the healer transform that rickety, senile person into this tall, stately man?" Alma asked, overwhelmed.

"The easiest way for me to explain it would be if Earth took all mystic yogis and put them into one superior being, they might come up with a prehistoric Kredon healer," Jetron explained.

"The healer uses no devices or drugs; only the powers of his mind. There is no cloaking game—no hypnosis to make you think you're seeing something other than the real image. You should spend some time with the healer to learn more, Xidiea," he concluded.

"You haven't changed a bit from when I was a boy, Bejion," Mark proclaimed. "Well, that's not entirely true. There wasn't even a hint of gray in your hair back then," he said smiling. "Welcome home."

"It's so good to be home, master Hemlon," Bejion said. "It's hard for me to accept that you and Miss Xidiea are all grown up."

"Why don't we go into the next room," Jetron said, motioning the group toward PRETOR's domain. "Do you still have your memories from Ecko?" he asked Bejion as they walked.

"Yes. The healer would never be able to remove those scars. Although I admit, after a time went by and I realized there was no leaving the place, I made myself a home. No one else knows the place as I do. I could identify every single rock and brick within the whole structure," Bejion said sadly.

They entered the ultra-modern chamber where intelligence was challenged against the computer. PRETOR's specific domain fed a network of terminals and scanners throughout Cralic Sector and the other inhabited places on Kredo.

Jetron motioned the group to sit. He commanded the computer to record the session.

"Bejion, do you recall any conversations that Asedi may have had pertaining to allies, hiding places; any plans that he made in case he had to leave Kredo, Ecko or Neverron?" Alma asked.

"There are places on Ecko that I haven't been to. I did overhear stories from the guards about places where Asedi might go that would be difficult to track. Underground structures with well-hidden entrances. There are also allies on distant planets: Uger, Destron, Soldane. Those would be good hiding places, and his friends most likely have other hiding places we know nothing about," Bejion explained.

"We should have PRETOR send ganji across the surfaces of Kredo and Ecko with Asedi's bio-chem analysis. They'll locate him if he is on or below the surface," Mark stated.

"Yes, that would do. PRETOR, display the bio-chem analysis of Asedi, Keeper of the Keys," Jetron commanded.

A three-foot square screen popped up projecting the requested information. A photo image of the villain appeared next with general statistics.

"Distribute the bio-chem analysis of Asedi to the ganji. Search superstructures and subterranean structures on

Kredo and Ecko. Seize and transport the subject back to Cralic Sector. Deny all privileges to this subject. That is all," Jetron ended.

"Where are the boys?" Mark asked. The last time they had gone off, trouble followed. He didn't want a repeat performance.

"Cordro is keeping them busy. They are eager to learn about Kredo, especially the growing facilities," Jetron said. He had been amused at their incessant questions about the different floors in the building.

"That was the first place they projected to, and they've been captivated by them ever since," Mark replied. "They caught Preston and Spencer off-guard when they displayed their abilities."

Alma stood and turned to the others. "I shouldn't leave here yet, but I'm uneasy about our Earth home. Mark, I am going to send the Ruar staff back there. Please alert Preston, Spencer, and Cook about the impending danger. Tell them the Guardian of Ruar will be there," she said.

She grasped the black staff with both hands and stared through it. Within minutes her hands were empty. The mission was in progress.

Mark pressed a button on the right control panel arm of the chair. He produced an alpha-symbolic keyboard that held no similarity to the industry standard of Earth. He keyed in a detailed message, then pressed a final button which sent the message to their Earth home.

The trusted servants soon would be alerted of any danger, and they would be aware of the Guardian's visit.

His part done, Bejion left the three behind to join Cordro and the young charges. With the healing, he was able to blend into the life that had been familiar to him many years ago.

Bejion didn't want to get embroiled with political matters anymore. Look what it had done to him before! He shook his head and walked down the corridor and out of sight.

"They're not going to find him," Alma said, pacing slowly. "He has found a secret place, I know it."

"Search deep within yourself, Alma. Where does that thought come from?" Mark asked, leaving the chair to go to her. He held her face tenderly and looked into her eyes, searching for the information.

Mark longed to make love to her at that instant. He restrained himself and helped by plying her with questions that would lead her to answers.

"Go to the energy from Ruar. Use it to find that thought, Alma," he coaxed.

Interested in this exchange, Jetron sat quietly and observed his two favorite people. This was new to him.

Although they had been betrothed since Alma's birth, and both families had considered them as a unit, Alma had been sent away out of harms reach as an infant.

Hemlon had always been close by, an observer at times, a participant at others. What joy he experienced to see them together as they should have been many years ago.

Noticing his son-in-law's use of his daughter's Earth name, Jetron decided that the name suited her. If it pleased her, he would address her by that name.

The transition had been difficult for her and he determined that a simple thing such as a name shouldn't cause major problems.

The future looked keen with the family reunited. A reclaimed friendship emerged with the return of his long-lost friend and advisor, Bejion, and soon the door would close on the ugly mess with Asedi.

A whole new challenge was forthcoming with the subject of superior intelligence, and the next generation—his grandsons.

BEEP, BEEP, BEEP.

The computer blasted into the quiet room, interrupting private musings.

"What are your findings, PRETOR?" Jetron asked as the monitor popped up from the smooth surface.

"The subject in question is not available at this time," PRETOR chimed. "Do you request another search?"

"Yes. I want all known associates of the subject brought to the regenerating facilities. When all are gathered, run a bio-chem analysis on each. That is all," Jetron dismissed.

"What level will you regenerate their minds to, Jetron?" Mark asked.

"Menial task accomplishment, level two. I don't want idiots; morons will do just fine. We won't have to worry about them being influenced by corruption. I hate having to do this, but most of them are hardened criminals and are easily bribed," Jetron explained.

"What good would prison be when they have so many avenues of corruption around them? They would be intolerable to the other inmates, and I'm sure they would band together once again to instigate an uprising on Ecko. We don't need that. I still have to appoint a new keeper."

"Mark, send the ganji to the places where Bejion said Asedi had friends. We must return home as soon as possible, I have an uneasy feeling about something and I can't quite understand what it is," she said. "Can we leave the boys here for a while, father?"

"Of course, Alma. They would be safe here, and well attended, and I want to get to know them better," Jetron said.

Mark smiled at the use of the Earthbound name. He instructed PRETOR on the new task, wondering if Alma had caught her father's subtle change.

Chapter 19

Alma knew her sons would be safe, and she was comfortable with leaving the boys at Cralic Sector. Mark had instructed PRETOR to attach a ganji to each son, and the entire community was alerted to possible danger. The people of Kredo were not about to let anything happen to Reena's grandsons.

The glittering transformation of molecules and energy was like millions of diamond chips twinkling. Their sharp, clear color was similar to the parting that Mark and Alma took from PRETOR's room.

It happened every day on Star Trek re-runs.

Although a month ago she never would have dreamed anything so fantastic for her future.

Without the bulk and clumsiness of vessels, the trip was startlingly fast. There was no worry of fuel, breakdowns, crew members, provisions or the many other endless things to consider.

Why hadn't they projected this in those futuristic TV shows and movies?

She wondered about these things as she whizzed through space with her companion beside her. The only thing that came close to Kredon power was *Star Wars*, or the movie

Starman. And even he had to use a vehicle and those tiny orbs.

Earth. The beauty of the planet was breathtaking with its white swirls of clouds and the deep blue of the seas. She wondered if others out there were observing from a distance and appreciated this beauty. When she and Mark ripped through the atmosphere and closed the distance, she was curious to know if they appeared as blips on a radar screen. Wouldn't the UFO groups love that!

Home. They would soon be back at the house; another blink of the eye and her feet would be on the ground and she could rejoin her Earth body once more.

Where was home, really?

She was pulled toward each place.

Would she ever place more of a kinship to one than the other?

Alma allowed her mind to play with her troubled questions.

"Alma, we should aim to arrive in the safe room," Mark said, interrupting her solitude. He didn't want her to pick up on his concern of the unfinished premonition she had had on Kredo.

If anything had happened to her Earth form...

As they materialized, Mark controlled the situation. "Do not open the door yet, Alma. Let me summon Preston to see if all is well."

Mark was whole once more. Alma remained a glittering form until she could merge with her Earthbound body. If she had begun this trek from Kredo instead of Earth she would not experience this merging problem.

Imagery travel by Kredons from the home world was a simple process. One merely stepped aside from the body, then used a mind bubble to condense the form into a tiny orb placed in a safe place until the person returned.

Alma looked forward to the time that she wouldn't need to worry about a solid human form when she traveled. Mark would envelope her in a bubble to take her to Kredo, as Asedi had done to the boys, so the problem would be eliminated.

The door slid smoothly, silently open, then closed after Preston entered the room.

"Master Mark! Miss Alma! We were all relieved to hear that you were well and together once again. Are the boys at Cralic Sector?" he jabbered, looking past them for the young travelers.

"It is good to be home again, our home away from home, eh Preston?" Mark smiled. "What is the situation? Is the Guardian of Ruar here? Is everything in order?"

Silently, he asked Preston *have there been any disturbances? Is my wife's body still safely hidden in the garden room?*

"Yes, the Guardian is here; everything seems to be fine," he replied, aloud. Preston continued the silent exchange with his master.

The mistress can return to her body, it has been well-protected. We worried constantly that something would go wrong ever since you sent that message. We shouldn't stall any longer, she will suspect something is amiss and there is no need to cause her more concern.

"I'm anxious to be whole again. Your feet are firmly planted on the ground," Alma reminded them. "It's my turn now."

They left the lab which no longer seemed unusual since her trip to Kredo and all that had transpired in the short period. As they approached the garden room, an overwhelming source of live energy surged out to Alma.

When they entered the large, airy room, rolling fog covered the floor. Directly beside the place where Alma's body sat invisible to the naked human eye, stood the Guardian of Ruar in his tall, icy splendor.

Alma was compelled—drawn to his presence by such a force that there was no holding back. Gliding across the room, her hands reached out automatically as he greeted her with the great staff.

She knowingly grasped the gleaming black staff placing one of her hands beside each of his icy hands. Their hands wedged together perfectly on the powerful rod, fitting snugly like interlocking puzzle pieces.

"Daughter of the stars, gift to the Earth. Welcome," he said. His words triggered her release; she staggered back a few steps, crackling with his gift of energy. "Return to your form quickly."

Spencer and Cook silently watched as the three entered the room. They made eye contact with their master and Preston. Like watching a play unfold, the audience was held spellbound, caught up with the suspense.

Alma returned to the place where her Earth form sat waiting and rejoined it without any difficulty. In minutes, she stood, her leggings and shirt looking as meticulous as if they had just been laundered, replacing the garment from Kredo.

After acknowledging the others present, Alma turned to the ice figure of the Guardian. "What is the link that binds us? You are neither of Earth nor Kredo, yet there seems to be a current that links me to you," she stated.

"There is no need to question your parentage. You are yet a babe in developing your intelligence and power, a thousand millennia away from where you shall be one day. I have waited patiently, watching over you through these developing years on Earth with your guardians.

"I was concerned, at first, with your simple life, then understood the charade as the clues became apparent. You were being protected. My race has dwindled rapidly over the past thousand years. We are but a small handful now, making our worlds where we choose to observe others. Our kind constantly search for a superior intelligence to train in our wake."

He hesitated a minute then nodded to Mark. "If your Kredon scientists had perfected genetic tracking, they would marvel at their choice of marriages. As it is, the odds were more than a million to one that such a genetic marriage could be more perfect.

"This marvel did not begin with you two. The joining of your parents in marriage started the process. They each possessed superior genetic qualities that enhanced your births. Your betrothal as children, and finally, your marriage surpassed the genetic expectation.

"The outcome was not what we expected, but rather, a twist of circumstances. The male of the species is usually the dominant force in power and intelligence; in your family, with your genes, we are seeing significant changes in the intelligence level of the female gender.

"You, Alma-Xidiea, are exorbitantly more intelligent and gifted than your husband, who is at the highest level of intelligence among Kredons. And you have not developed to your full capacity.

"If you two particular people were to create a female child, the babe would be crippled with the lack of proper training. Earth is centuries behind Kredo, which is centuries behind Ruar. We will train you so that you may train your sons, and your female child, if you conceive one," he stated.

"Was the surge of energy from the staff such a training session?" Mark asked, astounded by the information from the Guardian.

"No, that was a simple statement toned down as low as I could make it," the Guardian replied. "I am sure you noticed while you were training your wife that she was very adept at picking up certain lessons. After her simple Earth life, you would assume the lessons would be more difficult for her to grasp. As it stands, they are simple challenges.

"The universe is abundant with interesting life forms all in different development stages, all with different physical and mental shapes.

"Some life forms have a great deal of longevity; others are such short lifespans it doesn't seem practical to exist. Earthlings are increasing their lifespans but they are still so short, there is hardly enough time to develop properly.

"Ninety-eight percent of all humans of the planet Earth never reach full mental maturity before death. Most only use a tiny portion of their brains, and practically the whole race concentrates on developing the left hemisphere instead of the right. As time goes by, they will learn to develop that right side that stores all their dormant powers, just waiting to be put to use. Perhaps in another five-hundred years they will approach the threshold of true intelligence," the Guardian explained.

As the group listened, fascinated by the explanation from the strange being, an apparition appeared before them. The twisted, evil face peered through the gray hooded cloak, sneering at Alma.

"You beast!" Alma yelled as she raised an arm, clutching her fist tightly.

"Ha ha ha ha ha!" Asedi screeched. "You don't think I am fool enough to let myself be captured, do you?" The maniacal laughter followed, echoing eerily throughout the room.

"Guardian, you tricked me! You promised that you would hold the man until I returned so I could punish him!" Asedi accused.

"You lied about the true purpose of your mission, therefore I was not obligated to continue guarding the Kredon that you chose to imprison," the Guardian replied. "The price that you will pay for this deceit is high; you will realize that you are but a mortal soul, and you will not be given another chance for another lifetime."

A snarl twisted the features outlined by the dull hood; the man had clearly crossed over the precipice of sanity. "All of you have tricked me for the last time! Now that you are together in one place I will destroy you!"

The icy hand of the Guardian held the opaque rod out in front of him. A wavering folded air surrounded the occupants of the room.

Asedi thrust his hand out in front of him. Several bursts of deadly energy shot out, encircling the wavering group, but they deflected and dissolved.

The evil maniac screamed in rage. "I will conquer Kredo! And when I do you will be my slaves!"

Asedi's image wavered and disappeared.

Breaths were released. The Guardians staff absorbed his protective field.

"There are many interesting aspects of life to study and understand in this universe. Once before, you questioned how one can suddenly become evil," the Guardian recounted.

"Evil is like a wisp of fog floating in the air. It becomes absorbed into the souls of discontented beings, growing and eating the goodness out of the soul. Before long, not a shard of goodness remains in the festered soul, and the being no longer belongs in a decent society.

"Where there are wars, murders and other crimes, evil lurks and grows. It remains until the society becomes advanced enough to learn how to cleanse the evil away. Kredo is close to accomplishing this. Earth, on the other hand, has many centuries to go before they understand that they can control such things."

Chapter 20

Morning lifted its eyelids across the sleepy horizon, bursting sunlight through the sheer, white lacy curtains that covered the wall of bedroom windows.

Turning on her back, Alma covered her eyes with an arm, refusing to leave her sleep-state. She was comfortable and warm; she moved her arm back a few inches and blinked, letting the sunlight penetrate them.

Scenes were still coursing through her brain. The landscape that her mind had caught and memorized was not from anything she could remember.

She vaguely recalled a computer and a strange sitting room. She allowed the pictures to continue rolling across her mind. There had been an enormous amount of activity in a short period of time.

Her back ached. Had she even slept, she wondered? As she lay there staring at the ceiling, the other occupant stirred from his deep abyss of sleep.

Alma turned on her side cuddling up to the warm muscled form with her arm across his well-formed chest. He mumbled senseless words from deep within his sleep and was instantly awakened by his own sounds.

He lay on his back with her warm body molded to his, while his left arm draped along the length of her hip.

"Morning," he said, sleep drifting away to allow the full function of his faculties to take over.

"Good morning," she said as she hoisted herself up on her side and kissed him. Her fingers feathered his unruly blond hair, then travelled down to his muscular chest. "Did you sleep well? I hardly slept a wink last night! Let me tell you about the dream that I had. It was so real."

High up in the blue sky powdered with immense white, fluffy clouds, a hooded evil face peered through its shadowed hiding place, watching. . . waiting.

The End

About The Author

Dawn Greenfield Ireland writes full time. She lives among dreams and fantasies with two cats and moving boxes. Her head is filled with stories. She doesn't suffer from writer's block. If you buy her books and products, she'll love you forever.

DawnGreenfieldIreland.com